A Very Brief Season

A Very Brief Season

Barbara Girion

Charles Scribner's Sons
NEW YORK

Library of Congress Cataloging in Publication Data
Girion, Barbara, 1937-
A very brief season.
Summary: Ten short stories chronicle the happy and
sad times of teenage life.
1. Short stories, American. [1. Short stories]
I. Title.
PZ7.G4398Ve   1984   [Fic]   84-1217
ISBN 0-684-18088-X

3 5 7 9 11 13 15 17 19 F/C 20 18 16 14 12 10 8 6 4 2

Printed in the United States of America

*F*OR BLANCHE TAUB WARREN, my very special mother, whose strength, wisdom, and love carried me safely through my own very brief season and have continued to guide and support me through the other seasons of life.

With love, Barbara Michelle

*T*HOUGH ADULTS TELL YOUNG PEOPLE, "Enjoy yourself! This is the best time of your life!" the teens in my stories often find this difficult to believe.

I remember thinking the same thing as I struggled with my own adolescence, trying to get along with my parents and have them understand me. Then there was the tight-rope walk where I tried to be an individual and at the same time felt the need to be exactly like all my friends. I'll always remember the fear, wonder, and joy of falling in love and praying that that certain someone would love me back.

Some days I would be so high and happy, and then suddenly sad and moody. Through it all there were the vague but special plans to be made for a future that seemed so far away.

But all too soon the highs were not so high and the lows were not so low, and I realized that I had made it. I'd survived and passed through the best and worst of that very wonderful, but oh so very brief, season. . . .

And now that I'm an adult, I find myself telling my young readers, "Enjoy yourself! This is one of the very best times of your life!"

Barbara Girion

Contents

With a Little Gold Pencil 1
Rip-Off! 13
A Very Brief Season 27
Trophy 49
To Francie, with Love 61
The Moon Cookies 75
King of the Hill 91
Next of Kin 107
Another Blue-Eyed Quarterback 121
The Makeover of Meredith Kaplan 135

With a Little Gold Pencil

I HAD BEEN A REPORTER FOR Union High's paper since my freshman year. Now, as a junior, I was features editor and doing everything possible to make sure I was appointed editor-in-chief for my senior year.

I knew that the way to keep ahead of the competition was to come up with super ideas, and this year I'd hit on a winner. I had started a personality news column called "Shelby Sez," with my picture at the top. That's me, Shelby Dreighton, age seventeen. I thought of myself as a high-school-age Barbara Walters, getting juicy interviews with a cross-section of the student body. No one was safe from me: jocks, cheerleaders, grinds, intellects, freaks. I would quote them and then write my own opinion of their activities.

Of course I wasn't always kind, and some of the things I said were slightly controversial. As a result, almost every week I had a fight with Mr. Harrington, our adviser—like the time he read my column on class do-gooders. I had said that do-gooders would even mop up the bathroom floors if they could put it on their college applications and get credit for being well-rounded students.

"Are you sure you want to write this, Shelby?" That was Mr. Harrington's favorite remark.

"Are you telling me I can't write it, Mr. Harrington?"

"Just remember, Shelby, you can do a lot of damage to a person with a little gold pencil."

He was referring to a *real* little gold pencil. It had been a gift to me from Mom and Dad. It was attached by a chain to a tiny refillable notebook, and I carried it everywhere. I try to make the person I'm interviewing feel comfortable. No tape recorders or big notebooks—just this tiny pencil and pad that fit neatly into my pocket. It's amazing, but when people see the pencil they're caught off guard. I don't think they realize you can write just as much with a little pencil as with a big one.

Of course I *did* get plenty of "Why don't you drop dead and save us the trouble of drowning you?" letters after the publication of some of my columns. But if that was the price of freedom of the press, so be it.

Now I was angling for a column on L. Mark Compton, super-jock, *the* athlete at Union High. A six-foot-two senior with incredible black eyes and eyelashes, he had letters in football, basketball, and track.

When I cornered L. Mark after his basketball practice one evening, he said he'd give me a couple of minutes. He had just showered, and there were still some drops of water sparkling in his hair. We sat in the bleachers and talked about sports and team spirit, and he told me how great it was to play for good old Union. But that isn't what Barbara Walters would settle for, and neither would I.

"Mark," I said. "Really, the kids like to read personal stuff. You know, your favorite foods, rock stars, TV programs . . . stuff like that."

He hesitated. When he did speak, his voice was low and soft. But I wasn't supposed to be lulled by his voice. I was supposed to be concentrating on his words. If I didn't, Larry would say, "I told you so."

That's Larry Williams. He's a senior and editor-in-chief. We've been sort of going together this year. He keeps saying I've got the best chance at editor-in-chief because I'm completely professional. He also said I was the only one he'd trust to interview L. Mark Compton, because every other girl on the paper would immediately fall in love with him.

Mark stood up. "Listen, Shelby Dreighton, I've read some of the interviews you've done with other kids. I'm not about to give you any ammunition."

That annoyed me. Besides, I was beginning to feel uncomfortable. He was just so big standing there. Every once in a while our knees would touch, and those beautiful eyelashes were very distracting.

I looked down at my notebook. My little gold pencil had been drawing flower petals. I *never* doodle during interviews. I flipped to a fresh page.

"Everybody calls you Mark, but your name is L. Mark. Tell me, what's the first initial for?"

"No, you don't. That's my secret." He reached for his gym bag. "But I'm starving, and I'll buy you a burger. My car's in the lot."

That's how the interview began. In fact, it took a while for it to end. It lasted through three evenings—*great* evenings, I should add. Of course I got a razzing from Larry, especially when I broke our weekly Friday night date to watch Channel 10's movie greats so I could sit in the bleachers and cheer for Union High and L. Mark Compton.

"I think you're falling for that guy, like every other girl in this school," Larry said.

"Wrong!" I retorted. "Didn't you ever hear of research?"

"Research at a basketball game?"

"If you want me to write about L. Mark Compton, I've got to observe him in his natural habitat, don't I?"

That Friday, after the game, I waited for L. Mark. When he came out of the locker room, he steered me out of the gym and out to the parking lot—through a maze of kids, including the cheerleaders, who lifted their eyebrows. I felt quite aglow from all the looks we got.

After going for pizza, we sat in front of my house in Mark's car and talked. He had his arm draped over the back of the seat and was talking in that low voice, and Barry Manilow was singing something on the radio—I don't know what. All I knew was that L. Mark was awfully near and that the music was making me feel very drifty. Mark was talking about the ocean, saying that he was a certified scuba diver and that every summer he worked on a university oceanography project. He wanted to major in marine biology in college. It really surprised me.

I don't know how I concentrated, though. The music kept sending vibrations through the car. Or maybe *I* was sending them. All of a sudden L. Mark leaned over and kissed me.

There are some things you can't report even if you *are* a super-objective reporter. I floated into the house, and all I know is that for the next few days, every time I heard Barry Manilow on the radio, my mind just seemed to drift away from whatever I was trying to concentrate on. Of course Larry noticed and started to kid me about it, and about the fact that I hadn't yet done my "Shelby Sez" column on L. Mark Compton.

"Don't worry," I said. "You'll have it on your desk by Friday."

The next day I waited for Mark outside the gym even though we didn't have a definite date. He walked out with some of the guys and sort of lit up when he saw me. "Hi, Shelby!" he said. "Hey, grab this, will you?" He had his gym bag in one hand and tossed me his loose-leaf notebook with the other—expecting *me* to carry it! I couldn't believe it! That did it. I'd had enough of Larry's taunts, for one thing, but for another I realized maybe Larry was right: Mark just took it for granted that every girl would fall for him. But not me.

He drove me home, and right in the middle of a Barry Manilow record, I leaned over and said, "C'mon, L. Mark. You know all my ambitions, and I know yours. Aren't you ever going to tell me what the L. stands for?"

He didn't even hesitate. Big, strong L. Mark trusted me. "Lancelot," he said.

"What? I don't believe it! Lancelot, like in King Arthur?"

"The same. My mother was a nut on lovers in literature. You know, Lancelot and Guinevere. So she promised herself that her first son would be named Lancelot. Luckily, my father insisted on adding Mark, too."

"Fantastic story." I leaned back against my seat. "Maybe you're lucky she didn't fall in love with *Gone With the Wind*. She could have named you Rhett."

"I've thought of that. Or Cyrano, from *Cyrano de Bergerac*."

"Or Count Vronsky, from *Anna Karenina*?"

We played this game all the way home. I should have realized that we were picking only ill-fated lovers.

Lancelot Mark Compton never said a word when the "Shelby Sez" column appeared. It began with a question:

"Guess what a fantastic, three-letter athletic hero's first initial, L, stands for? Not love—though you'd think so, from the lineup of girls at the locker room—but for Lancelot! Please tell us, Lancelot Mark Compton: Could it be that Mark is really for Mark Antony, as in *Antony and Cleopatra?*"

He never said a word when he stood on the foul line that night and missed because the opponent's crowd was hooting, "Lancelot, Lancelot, trot back home to Camelot. . . ."

He never said a word when his locker was decorated with big red paper kisses and a sign saying, "To Lancelot, love from Guinny and all the other maids-in-waiting." As a matter of fact, he never said a word about it because Lancelot Mark Compton apparently had decided never to speak to me again.

I resumed my Friday nights at the TV movies with Larry, but it wasn't the same. First of all, Larry's kisses were getting a little too demanding. And frankly, they were boring. Kissing Larry had never been boring before. But of course I hadn't had L. Mark's kisses to compare them with. Larry couldn't help but notice. I tried to kiss him good-night with a little enthusiasm, but I couldn't manage it.

"Look, Larry," I finally said, "let's cool it a little, okay? I mean, we work well together on the paper, and I don't think we should mess up the relationship with all this other stuff."

"What's up, Shelby? Is it still Mark Compton? I thought that Lancelot column meant your crush was all over."

"There's nothing to be over 'cause there was never anything to begin with. Right now I'm just interested in becoming editor-in-chief and doing a good job for the paper."

"Okay by me." He zipped up his jacket.

I leaned over and kissed him on the cheek. Larry really was a nice guy, and I didn't want him to be mad. "You know, Larry, I'll tell you something if you promise not to laugh. Ever since I was a little girl, I've just wanted to be another Brenda Starr."

"Brenda Starr . . . like in the comics?"

"I know it's silly, but I always thought she was a real person and I wanted to be just like her, writing fabulous stories, being a famous reporter, traveling, wearing glamorous clothes, meeting mysterious men—the whole bit."

He opened the door. "Just think," he said. "When I was a little kid, I only wanted to be a fireman."

The next week, besides my column—in which I got in a dig about all the expensive student cars in the parking lot—I had to write a long, boring story about the guidance department. Larry excused me from putting the paper to bed, since I was already swamped with all the data from my research.

On Friday morning, when the paper came out, I didn't get to pick up my copy because I was busy making up labs I had missed while trying to make sense out of the guidance department. After lab, as I walked down the hall to my locker, I heard a lot of snickers and also noticed Paul Mann, one of the school's biggest nerds, standing near my locker with a bunch of his pals. They were all talking at once. I knew they were still mad about my story on them, in which I remarked that they gave Union some of the trashy aura of the New York Bowery.

"Well, if it isn't Brenda Starr. . . ." "Yeah, how ya doin', Brenda?" "Say, looking for a mystery man, Brenda?" "How about me?"

Paul got down on his knees. "Hey, Brenda, I'll put a patch on my eye if it'll turn you on."

"What are you talking about?" I asked, really annoyed. I took a step toward my locker. On the door was a note the size of a poster: "Dear Brenda: Never realized you wanted a little love in your life. I'll meet you tonight. Your mystery man."

The hoots got louder. One of the girls from the paper was going by, and I pulled her over. My cheeks were getting hot. I didn't like being laughed at. "Hey, Gail, what's going on?"

"Oh Shelby!" she said, laughing. "Didn't you see your interview? It was a fabulous idea!"

"My interview? What are you talking about?"

Gail handed me the school paper and pointed to the "Shelby Sez" column. Instead of my story on the cars in the parking lot, there was a story about me! "That famous Union High School girl reporter—who, with her little gold pencil, cuts down personalities like a machete in a sugarcane field—has revealed to your editor-in-chief that she's always dreamed of being Brenda Starr. In fact, this girl reporter, obviously still arrested in an adolescent state, has even shown evidence lately that she would be receptive to a mystery man! Any mystery men out there? Your reporter awaits you. . . ." And so on. I felt sick. How could Larry take something I had told him privately and print it like that? And how could he distort it so much and make me look and sound like such a fool? I found my way to the girls' room. I didn't want to cry, but I couldn't help it. I flushed the toilet every time someone walked in so no one would hear me. I made myself wash my face, smile, grit my teeth, and last through a horrible day of taunts.

Late in the afternoon I passed Mark Compton. Well, I

thought, I'm surely going to hear from him. He just smiled and said, "Hi, Shelby," as he passed by. That was the first time he had spoken to me since his interview.

I couldn't sleep the whole night. I had a lot of thinking to do: about interviewing people and making news at the expense of others.

Monday afternoon we had a newspaper staff meeting. I knew everyone was watching me, especially Larry and Mr. Harrington. I didn't say anything, except when Larry asked if anyone had some new ideas to offer.

I raised my hand. "I've got one, Larry." I looked around the table. "I'd like to do something different for the 'Shelby Sez' column. I'd like to spend some time each week actually participating in the activity of the person I'm writing about—like working with the prom committee, or practicing with the fencing club, or studying with the grinds."

There were murmurs around the table. Larry leaned over and whispered something to Mr. Harrington and then looked back at me.

"What exactly is the point, Shelby? First of all, it'd take an awful lot of extra time, and second, I don't see how it could have any real impact on the column." Some of the other kids nodded.

I cleared my throat. "Well, what I have in mind is giving the column a new slant, some new life. But even more important, well . . . I've been doing a lot of thinking, and I have a feeling that if I were more *involved* in what I wrote about, maybe I'd really understand the things other kids are interested in—instead of just putting them down."

Mr. Harrington smiled, and I knew I had another winner.

"Okay, sounds good to me," Larry said. "Go to it."

When the meeting ended Larry walked over to me and held my arm. "So, what's the first 'new' column going to be about, Shelby?"

"It's going to be a surprise," I answered. I pulled my arm away, but gently. "I'll tell you this much, though: It *is* going to take lots of 'practice.' But don't worry about my meeting the deadline—I'm starting the story right away."

"Okay, I'm counting on you!" Larry said with a smile. He headed down the hall.

Before starting for my next class, I pulled out my little gold pencil and wrote a reminder to myself: "Talk to L. Mark's basketball coach about getting hold of an extra uniform, my size." Then I drew a little flower petal next to the note.

Rip-Off!

*M*Y PARENTS WERE really on my back this year: marks, S.A.T.'s, extracurricular activities. I thought I'd go nuts. Dad became an expert on college enrollment, and Mom studied lists of available scholarships as if they were the Bible.

Amy Barnett was stretched across my bed. "You're really lucky, Amy," I said.

"Why, Jen?"

"Because you're all set with nursing school. No more hassle."

"It's not that I'm so lucky. It's just that I've always wanted to be an old bedpan carrier, marry a rich doctor, and live happily ever after—like in the good old days when our mothers were young. And you want to discover a new geometric formula or whatever the heck you're into."

I turned over on my back. "I am just so tired of reading catalogs and making decisions."

Amy threw over her car keys. They landed on my stomach. "Let's go to the mall. Come on, you drive."

That was another thing I liked about Amy. She knew how to pull me out of moods. We had become close friends just this year. I had always been too busy studying to hang around with people before.

Amy's father took the train to work, so she usually had the family car. And the mall was a good place to meet some kids, rap a little. We drifted in and out of stores. We were in a cosmetic department, and I was fooling around, spraying myself with perfume samples, trying some lipsticks and eye shadows, when a salesgirl walked over. "Help you with anything?"

"I'm just looking."

She closed the open lipstick and pushed the perfumes toward the back of the counter.

"These are for sampling, aren't they?" I asked.

"Yes, but you kids mess them all up and then it's hard to tell the colors." She took a tissue and rubbed some blue out of the green eye shadow.

Kids? I'm seventeen. I don't know who she was talking about. She couldn't have been much older herself.

I reached across the counter for Summer's Delight and sprayed myself—my hair, behind the ears, my wrists. I even waved it back and forth across my chest for good measure.

"Hey!" The salesgirl walked back to me. "That's powerful stuff! You're supposed to use just a little."

Stuff it! I said to myself. I pushed the bottle back across the counter.

I waited for Amy outside. "Let's get a hamburger," I said when she came out. "I've got about ninety-seven cents. Maybe we can splurge for some fries."

"You smell as if you belonged in a French bordello!"

"I smell like Summer's Delight," I said, "and what do you know about bordellos?"

"I take that back. You smell like a massage parlor on 42nd Street in New York City."

"Again I ask, what do you, Amy Barnett, Florence Nightingale's reincarnation, know about massage parlors?"

"Aha, I know about a lot of things!" She reached into the jacket of her windbreaker and pulled out one of those little boxes that hold panty hose. "*Voilà!*" She pulled another from the pocket on the other side.

"Why didn't you get it put in a bag?"

"Oh come on, Jen." She started to laugh. "You don't ask for a paper bag when you're taking something."

"You mean you *stole* them?"

"Oh, for Pete's sake! I should leave you home to molder with your isosceles triangles. I didn't steal them, I took them. Everybody does."

"But the store—what if they saw you?"

"Of course they didn't see me. They never do. What do you think I am, crazy? Besides, if they did, I'd just say I forgot to pay for them."

She handed me one of the panty hose containers. "One size fits all—here's one for you."

I hesitated. "For Pete's sake, don't make a federal case!" Amy stuffed the box in my pocket. "Those stores are insured up to their elevators. It's no loss to them. Let's go over to Snacktime."

I forgot about the stockings until a few days later. I had to give an oral report in biology and I wanted to wear a skirt. Every pair of panty hose seemed to have runs in it. Then I remembered Amy's present and put them on.

I had two interviews coming up with the top college choices on my list. Mother had gotten letters of recommendation from our minister, our family doctor, the director of the youth choir, and even my orthodontist—and my braces have been off for three years! Sometimes I wondered who was going to college—she or I.

On Saturday Amy and I went to the city. Dad had gotten us tickets for a hockey game. It was an extra belated birthday present for me. We shopped in the morning. I kept watching Amy, wondering if she was going to *take* any-thing. We were looking at little silk scarves. I opened one up. It would be dynamite with jeans and my red T-shirt. I looked at the price. That was dynamite, too. I backed away.

We got on the elevator to go up. Amy punched me. "Look in my pocket." She had on her good winter coat with the deep side pockets. I couldn't believe it: There was the plaid silk scarf I had just looked at. I broke into a sweat. I had never liked elevators anyway, but this was too much. My head was spinning. I felt as if I was about to lose my stomach, and the smell of people just closed around me.

When the elevator stopped, I wouldn't let Amy get out. "We're going back down," I told the operator. I didn't take a breath until we were through the main floor and out on the street.

Amy was laughing. "You are the biggest baby. You wouldn't take your head out of books for three years study-ing for college. And now that you go out, you don't know how to have fun!"

"But Amy, how can you do it?"

"Oh, it's easy." She handed me the scarf. "Courtesy of Busby's department store." She reached into her other pocket and pulled out a pair of fur-lined leather gloves. They looked expensive. She ripped the tags off and put them on.

She reached inside her coat and held up a cardboard square holding two hand-painted barrettes. "Do you like these?" I shook my head. But I took the price tag off the scarf.

She looked at the barrettes and then chucked them in a

garbage can. "I don't know. They looked nice in the store, but out here they're kind of tacky."

I looked back at the garbage can. That seemed like such a waste. Why rip them off if you were going to throw them away?

We enjoyed the game. The score was close, and the crowd was great. During the break after the first period, I walked up for refreshments. Talk about rip-offs! They charged seventy-five cents for a container of that really sweet iced tea that leaves you even thirstier when you're finished. It was very crowded, and I had to scream to be heard. "Two iced teas!" I handed the guy $1.50. As I turned I knocked over a stack of chocolate bars. It's hard to say what happened next. I was picking up the bars with the two iced teas in one hand and the straws in my mouth, and instead of putting the last chocolate bar on top of the pile, I dropped it in my pocket.

I walked back to the seat expecting a hand on my shoulder any minute. There was none. I gave Amy her iced tea and half the chocolate bar. I couldn't eat my half. It stuck to the roof of my mouth. I couldn't chew it. Or swallow it. I mean, it just stayed at the back of my throat. I took a sip of iced tea to help wash it down, and I felt the stickiness of it, all the way down to the pit of my stomach. I threw the piece still left in the wrapper on the floor.

I had a lousy week. Mother dragged me to a Women's Club meeting at the church. She introduced me to Mrs. Kopet, who was alumnae chairperson for Wellesley, one of the schools on my list. Mother just rattled away, and I couldn't get a word in edgewise. ". . . and Jennifer has been vice-president of the Modern Dance Club since her freshman year, and she writes for the school newspaper. She's really well rounded!" As if she had measured me with a compass. Mom was driving me bananas with this college stuff.

I didn't really want Wellesley. I wanted State University, but I didn't tell Mrs. Kopet that. State University was on the bottom of Mom's list. I'd just have to pray that Wellesley would reject me.

On Saturday Daddy asked me to have his tennis racket restrung. I called up Amy, and she went to the mall with me. We tried on some tennis clothes while we waited. Amy had on a cute Chris Evert dress with ruffled panties. The dress went back on the hanger. She pulled her jeans on over the panties. I sweated as the salesgirl took the dresses back. "Are you taking any of these?"

"No," answered Amy. "They don't fit right." Then she whispered so loudly in my ear that I thought everybody would hear, "and besides, the ruffled pants itch!" The salesgirl never noticed a thing. We got the racket and walked out laughing.

We headed back to Mandel's. Amy tried some black kohl around her eyes at the cosmetics counter. A salesgirl walked over. "Let me show you how to use that," she said. She wiped Amy's face with a tissue. I walked over to a large display case of purse-size bottles of perfume. There were four empty slots in the display case. I looked around. No one was noticing an honor student who was just about to be accepted at Wellesley College. There were five empty slots when I walked back to Amy.

"Amy, I don't feel well. Let's go."

"Just a minute, Jen. I want to see how this works."

I had just said that to get out of the store, but now I really didn't feel well. My hands were sweating, and there was a woman standing on the other side of the counter who I was sure was staring. I thought of Mom and her reference letters: "Jennifer, competition today is so keen you have to have absolutely impeccable references. They check way back to grade school."

"Amy, I'm going to be sick. Please." I didn't wait. Amy followed me. The cool air hit my face, and I started to breathe again. I ran to the car and waited for her to start it. We drove out of the lot and onto the highway. Suddenly I felt fine.

"What the heck was the matter with you?"

I didn't answer. I just pulled out the bottle of Gardenia perfume.

"Hey, neat!" said Amy. "Spray me." I did. And then I sprayed myself. The car was too small. We started coughing and laughing from the sweetness. We both opened our windows. "Wow, I'm going to have to air these seats out— it smells like a funeral parlor!" We laughed all the way home. When I said I had some reading to do, I didn't mind, for once, when she teased me about being a bookworm.

I put the bottle on my dressing table next to a stack of paperback books. I straightened the books and felt kind of funny. We always bought our books and newspapers from Mrs. Peterson, who ran the candy store in the center of town. Now she was selling out. Her husband had died a couple of years ago, and the store was too much for her. Kids were always ripping her off—greeting cards, gum, books, candy, anything they could get their hands on. Daddy had said her insurance just couldn't cover her losses.

It was a shame. I picked up the perfume and put it in my top drawer. It wasn't the same thing. Taking something from a big store—well, it wasn't like the little punks stealing from Mrs. Peterson. I mean, even Amy had said the big stores expected a certain amount of shoplifting. They added it into their prices right from the beginning.

It was waiting time for most of the senior class. Some kids had heard from schools—early acceptances, early rejections. I was happy when there was no mail addressed to me.

At dinner one night Daddy asked me if there was any news yet. News in our house meant one thing. College!

Mom interrupted. "By the way, college girl, Mrs. Kopet asked me today if you had heard anything yet. I told her we were still waiting." *We* were waiting! I suddenly lost my appetite.

Two weeks later Amy and I drove over to the mall. Amy had heard that some guys from the basketball team were supposed to be fitted at the sports store for team jackets. She was hoping to run into Tom Wiener. My own love life was pretty low at the moment. It was sort of in a holding pattern, like the rest of me. My boyfriend, Stan, had started college this year. We wrote, but he wouldn't be home for a while. Now that we were away from each other, I realized that we had stuck together for three years because we didn't have anybody else to be with.

Amy and I stood around the sports store awhile but didn't see anybody. We drifted back to Mandel's. Amy wanted to look at earrings. She always called me chicken, but I had held her hands when she had her ears pierced a few weeks ago. It was time to change the gold training posts.

I walked around the corner. A lady was looking at gold chains. They were laid out on a piece of black velvet, so I knew they must be expensive. Three were on one side, and she was looking at two more in the center. One of the three caught my eye. It was gold and had tiny seed pearls every few inches between the gold links.

Amy called from the other side, "Hey Jen, come back. I want you to help me pick." The salesgirl lifted her head as Amy called. It only took a second. I picked up the gold-and-pearl chain—I was wearing straight leg jeans tucked into boots—and dropped it straight down into my boot.

I walked over to Amy. I felt very calm. It was really a pretty chain. I'd tell Mom it was costume jewelry if she asked. You couldn't tell it was fourteen-carat unless you looked at the mark. Amy picked out a pair of gold hoops. They were costume jewelry. She paid and we left. We walked out into the parking lot.

"Just a minute there!" It was a deep, threatening voice. I stopped dead and felt myself begin to shake from the inside out.

"I've been watchin' you, young lady." I couldn't breathe. I turned around. There was a guy in his early twenties in jeans and a sweater. He took out his wallet and flashed a badge: "security agent for Mandel's."

I couldn't believe it. He looked just like an ordinary person, not a security agent. Good-bye Wellesley went through my mind. Then a stronger thought: Maybe good-bye State University? Maybe good-bye college? "Empty your pockets." He spoke with authority.

My God, what would Dad say? I wished for an earthquake, fire, something. I wished it were yesterday, I wished it were two hours ago. A half hour ago.

"Hurry up, I haven't got all day."

I put my hands in my pockets before I realized that he was talking to Amy.

"Hey listen, mister. I have these earrings." She waved the bag in his face. "See my receipt? I paid for these."

"I know what's in the bag. I'm interested in what's in your pocket."

I looked at Amy. Her face was very white, but her voice was still strong.

"Hey, I don't know what you mean."

"Back in the store, honey, and we're going to empty those pockets and see the goodies you've got."

She reached into her jacket. "Okay. Look, I took this other pair of earrings. That's all. Honest. Please, I never took anything before."

"Yeah, every kid I catch says the same thing. Sorry, honey, let's go back into the store."

Her voice was shaking now. "Please, I'll pay for them. I swear it was the first time. I meant to pay for them. I just slipped them in by mistake. Please give me a break."

"Let's go." He turned to me. "Your friend is going inside. I suggest you run along home and be careful who you hang out with before you're in trouble too."

Amy was crying. "Please." She was begging. "My mother will kill me."

"Well, we'll find out, because we're going to call her when we get inside."

He hadn't seen me! He had said I could go. Amy had her head in her hands. He hadn't seen! I could go. He didn't know. They'd caught her, they were going to call *her* mother!

He took her arm and walked her into the store. She

didn't say a word to me. I walked through the parking lot slowly, afraid to breathe. He might change his mind. Maybe he'd search me. Maybe someone else had seen me.

We had come in Amy's car. She had the keys; I'd have to walk home. I forced one foot in front of the other. Slowly. Don't run, I told myself. Someone will think it's suspicious.

I walked to the highway. There were woods on one side of the road. I walked on the curb. Cars were whizzing by me. There was a shortcut up ahead, through the woods. I had been warned since I was a little girl about drunks and perverts hiding in the woods. I took the path and as the woods closed around me I began to run. I ran until I had to stop to breathe. Then I reached into my boot and took out the chain—a thin gold chain with tiny pearls. I ripped it in half and then in quarters and then pulled the pearls off. I started running again, and as I ran I flung the pieces into the bushes on either side. I was saved!

The thought of State University or even Wellesley College had never been so good! I couldn't understand how I had gotten myself involved in all of this. Sure, I had been annoyed with my parents because they were on my back all the time. But was it my own fear at the thought of leaving home and everything familiar for college—any college—that had made me distract myself with cheap thrills? I hadn't just ripped off stores, I had almost ripped off my whole future.

The shortcut ended two blocks away from my house. I got home and into the bathroom without running into Mom. As I washed my face I noticed that my hands were bleeding from the ripped chain—thin, jagged lines where I had torn it apart across my palms. Fourteen carats are pretty strong. I traced one of the cuts with a finger. It trailed right into my lifeline, and the burning feeling reminded me that the scar would take a long, long time to fade.

A Very
Brief Season

*M*Y MOM AND I get along pretty well—most of the time, that is. We used to be at each other's throats all the time when I was younger, but now I'm a senior and almost seventeen so we try to work things out.

She went back to work when I was twelve. She was trained in art and now she's an artist's representative. She sells paintings and gets artists jobs illustrating magazines and books.

I can talk to Mom about things that are bothering me—trouble with boyfriends and girlfriends—and her advice is pretty good. Except when it comes to shopping expeditions.

Mom puts herself together terrifically. My friends think she's fabulous. She can take a plain old ordinary scarf and wrap it around her waist and twist it a few times and turn a whole outfit into something smashing. The trouble is she expects me to want to do the same thing.

I buy most of my clothes myself, but when I need something special Mom goes with me. And I do like her advice. She can go to the racks, leaf through them, grab a bathing suit that I would never have looked at, and say, "Here, Liz, try this one. It's perfect for you." And it usually is! I always worry about my stomach, which never is as flat as I want it, but the things she picks make it completely disappear.

My Uncle Larry was getting married in two weeks and Mom had set aside time to take me shopping. "Have your list ready, Liz. You know I don't like to waste time going from place to place." Mom is a "list" person. I guess that's why she's so efficient in her job, but it's a pain when you deal with her.

I already had a dress for the wedding. One of my older cousins had worn it to another wedding, and Mom had had it altered for me. It was light mauve with a high ruffled neck, long sleeves trimmed with matching ruffles, and a full skirt that spun and twirled at the slightest body movement. I wanted silver shoes, or gold—something to brighten up the dress. Mom hadn't answered when I mentioned the shoes, so I assumed we were on the same wavelength. I also needed jeans for school and a couple of long-sleeve shirts, and I thought we could do that much shopping easily.

First, though, I had to wait for Mom to get off the phone. I know her calls are important, but she never seems to care about *my* time. I just sat and waited, twirling one of my long pieces of hair until I had turned it into a perfect sausage curl. I have a long shag and it's very easy for me to keep. I wash it and pat it into place when I'm in a hurry or blow it back when I have more time. But Mom thinks I have too much hair. "It hides your features, Liz," she says. "Why don't you let me take you to Mr. Alexander and have it cut properly?"

That's another point of contention. We live in New Jersey, and Mom doesn't think that anybody in New Jersey can do anything. She has her hair cut and her nails done and buys all her make-up in New York City since we're only forty minutes away.

"You'll have to get rid of some of that hair when you

start college. You've had the same hairstyle for five years. Don't you want a different look?" To tell the truth, I could live with my hair another five years if necessary.

Mom finally finished her conversation and grabbed the car keys. "Let's go, Liz, before it rings again. Isn't this going to be fun? We haven't been shopping in a long time." She put her arm around my waist and planted a kiss on top of my head. I felt warm and cozy and protected. It was going to be fun. I crossed my fingers and promised myself that we wouldn't have any fights today.

Last night at dinner we had told Daddy about our shopping expedition. He threw up his hands. "Well, I think I'll work late at the office tomorrow. The last time you two went shopping, you snarled and spat at each other like alley cats for three days."

"Oh, don't be silly, Ted," Mom said. "That was when Liz was in one of her phases. We're all through with that."

I bristled at her words. It's always a "phase" when I have an opinion she doesn't like, but she always considers herself perfectly in control.

The minute we entered the junior department at the mall, it began. First Mom glanced at the ceiling, trying to find the speakers that put out the blaring rock music. "Why do they have to play it so loud? I'm going to have a headache before we even get started." She rubbed the back of her neck. "Well, let's get going and get out of here while I still have eardrums." I don't know why the music bothers her so; I hardly hear it. I guess that's because I always have music on while I'm getting dressed, taking a shower, or even studying.

I was looking for jeans, and Mom walked over to one of the racks. Before I could even blink, she held out a pair of navy blue wool slacks. "Liz, these would be great with your red-striped blouse, and we could get a matching blazer."

I stared at her. "Mom, nobody wears things like that to school."

"But you can wear them with so many things—a beautiful belt, a sweater. . . ."

"I'd be laughed out of the cafeteria. I need jeans."

"Well, you don't need me with you to buy jeans."

"Then I'll get a couple of pairs of straight leg corduroys."

"But you buy the same thing every year, and all your friends wear them. You always look as if you have on the same clothes."

"That's the way I want to look."

Mom approached a saleslady. "Where are the straight leg corduroys, please?"

"Across the aisle in the boys' department."

"In the boys' department?"

"Come on, Mom. Everybody buys pants there."

In the boys' department the saleslady rolled her eyes skyward in sympathy with Mom as I went through the racks.

"All the girls wear the boys' corduroys. We sell them out as fast as they come in."

I could see out of the corner of my eye that they were having a big discussion on how stupid teenage girls were, and I felt the back of my throat get tight. Finally I had an armful and we went into the dressing room. "These are great, Mom, and they fit perfectly."

"Well, the size seems okay. Let's go back and pick some colors."

"But Mom, I have all the colors I want."

She stared at the assortment I had brought into the

dressing room—a dull brown, khaki, a deep beige, and a pair that she picked up, saying, "This looks like dirty sand. How about a nice royal blue?"

I had one answer to that, a word I thought I had expunged from my vocabulary when I started studying for my S.A.T.'s: "Gross!"

"Or maroon. I think I even saw kelly green. Get a pair that has some color to it."

"Mom! Nobody wears those colors."

"Somebody must wear them. How come they're on the racks? These are practically interchangeable. You'll look as if you're wearing the same pants every day."

I stood my ground, the pants over my arm. "May I have the charge plate, please?"

Mom was not ready to give up until I reminded her of the expensive wool plaid slacks she had bought me early in the season. They occupied a permanent place in the corner of my closet, never worn. Round one to Elizabeth Jameson.

As we collected the packages and left the department, I spotted a booth with flashing red and blue strobe lights, featuring a young salesgirl who was transferring heat decals onto colored T-shirts.

"Oh Mom, let's stop."

"Liz, not another T-shirt. You must have four hundred of them at home. Let's get you some nice button-down oxfords that you can wear under sweaters when it gets cold."

I did have quite a collection at home. Crazy T-shirts were my specialty. I had them from colleges and rock concerts and from every vacation spot that anyone in my family had ever visited.

"There goes the music again." I watched Mom rub the

cord in the back of her neck. "Why do you have to look like every other teenager in America? Don't you want to be an individual? Don't you want to start getting together a nice wardrobe for college?"

"Half the teenagers in America wear button-down oxfords, Mom, but not in my crowd."

"When are you going to stop being just like every one of your friends? You're an individual. Do you think I'm like every suburban housewife? I went back to work and pursued my career."

"Let's go." I passed the booth without a backward glance. I was not into listening to Mom's speech number seventy-seven about how she'd pulled herself out of the rut all her women friends were in and had the strength to be an individual.

"Well, what else is on your list?"

"That's it." I glanced down at it quickly. "I'll go to the Army and Navy store for my jeans and pick up some shirts there."

"Liz, why did I bother to put this time aside if you're going to do the rest yourself?"

Uh-oh, speech number seventy-eight: how valuable her time was and how I, Elizabeth Jameson, had taken her away from clients who were hanging onto the telephone as if it were an umbilical cord, waiting for her to organize their lives. She did, too. Sometimes her artists had to appear at a lecture or on a TV program, and Mom would help dress them properly for the event.

"We still have to get the shoes," I said.

"Let's go." She glanced at her watch. "If we finish up with the shoes, we can have lunch, and then I can still salvage some of the day."

Again I felt that flash of resentment that always rose like a sour taste in the back of my throat.

"Let's go out into the mall to the shoe stores."

"Oh Liz, the shoes are so tacky in those shops. Let's look in a shoe department first."

I let her lead me up the escalator and into the carpeted area of the shoe floor. She sank gratefully into one of the chairs.

I started looking at the shoes lined up for display, picking them up and turning them over to check out the prices. I knew these shoes wouldn't be worn very often and was trying to find something in a low price range.

A salesman pulled one roughly out of my hand. "Please don't spoil the display. Ask for what you want."

If there's anything I hate, it's rude salespeople.

"Well, to tell you the truth, I don't see anything I want."

"Fine. Then just leave the samples alone."

I walked over to Mom. "They don't have anything. Let's go."

The salesman followed me over. With a start he took in Mom's sleek appearance, her slim pants suit and carefully done hair. He probably smelled her Paris perfume, too, because his manner changed completely. "Can I be of assistance, Madame?" He certainly knew in a second who held all the cards—the charge cards, that is.

Mom was all smiles. "Thank goodness you don't have that awful music blaring up here. Do you happen to have a nice plain high-heeled pump that could be dyed to match a sample?" She opened her bag and pulled out the silk sash to my dress.

"I didn't know you'd brought that with you, Mom."

"It's too hard to remember a color without a swatch."

The salesman was approaching with three pairs of plain silk pumps with different size heels.

"Any one of these will take the dye perfectly."

"Mom, can I speak to you for a moment?"

"What, Liz? These medium heels look very nice. Then we can pick up a pair of tinted stockings."

"Mom, that wasn't what I had in mind."

"No?" She wasn't really listening. The salesman had opened the dye color chart, and they were both comparing colors with the material swatch.

My eye caught something glittering in the corner. There, on a tiny mirrored table, were some metallic evening shoes. I picked up a gold pair with incredibly thin and very high heels. They were held together with crisscross straps that seemed to go across the instep and up the ankle like the laced sandals of ancient Roman gladiators. I turned them over. Size six, perfect. Slipping on the right shoe, I tied it around my ankle and hopped over to Mom and the salesman.

"This is it. This is the type of shoe I've been looking for."

They both looked at me, first at my face, then down at my feet. I guess I did look silly, one jean rolled up and the straps practically stopping the circulation in my foot. On my other foot I still had on my sneaker.

"Liz, for heaven's sake! Those are ridiculous. They'd be horrible with that dress. Take them off and let's get the pumps."

My little toe was feeling the pinch of the strap that was gripping it tightly, but the smug look on the face of the salesman hurt me even more.

"No," I said straight out, and sat myself in a seat. "Can

you please bring me the mate to this sandal so I can try it on?"

"Liz." Mom plopped herself down next to me. The salesman just stood there.

"Oh, bring her the mate," Mom said, "so she can see how ridiculous they look." She called after him—and Mom never raises her voice, especially not out of the confines of our house—"And bring a size six in the plain pumps, too, will you?"

Mom didn't say another word until the salesman came back. Neither did I. Every once in a while we kind of glared at each other, and she told me to fix my hair, which was standing up in the back.

I finally got both shoes on. They really were high, but I managed to stand up as straight as possible and walk across the floor. The straps cut not only into my little toes but into the fleshy part of my ankles. Still, I looked down from the added four inches of height and saw that the gold sparkled nicely.

"Go ahead, walk back and forth again." Mom waved me on in front of her. Thank goodness Smiley, the shoe salesman, had found someone else to hover over. He promised Mom he would return as soon as she needed him.

"I think they're terrific, Mom. I really like them. And Gram told me I could borrow her little gold evening bag, so that'll be perfect."

Mom lowered her head and kind of fiddled with her thumbs. "You know, Liz, I don't want to pull rank on you, but I really cannot believe you are serious about those shoes. You can barely stand up straight. They're biting into your flesh and make your ankles look as if you belong in a Minnie Mouse cartoon. Now surely you can see that."

She cleared her throat. "I realize that every once in a while you find it necessary to rebel, but I beg you, not over these shoes. They make you look, well, to tell you the truth, you look like a hooker, and a hooker whose feet hurt."

By this time I had the shoes off and was holding them protectively across my chest. It was as if Mom had pressed a button in my head. I felt my back stiffen and so did my will power. I was going to have these shoes no matter what Norma Jameson, sleek New York agent, thought. She didn't really care about me or about my friends or how I looked. She wanted one of those perfect little teens who exist on the pages of magazines, someone who could reflect her own good taste.

"Don't worry, Mom. If anyone asks me, I'll be sure to tell them that you had nothing to do with picking out these shoes. I'll even pin a sign on my back saying that Norma Jameson disowns the shoes her 'hooker' daughter is wearing."

Mom stood up and glanced at her watch. "I knew you were going to make one of your deals about this. You only want them because I told you they were terrible. I'll never learn. I should have told you they looked great, and then you would have heaved them over the edge of the escalator."

"So what are we going to do?" I stared at her.

"Right now we are going to have lunch." The salesman had rejoined us. Mom was terrific. She could have gotten an Academy Award. Her face smoothed over and she put on one of her most charming smiles, her voice soft and melodious. Only I recognized the cutting edge behind some of her words.

"We're going to try to have some lunch right now. Will you please hold these shoes?" Mom motioned to the gold sandals that I still clung to. "And a pair of the plain pumps in size six. We'll be back after lunch to make up our minds."

"I've made up my mind, Mom. Eating is not going to change it." She shot me a look from under lowered lids.

"Hand the man the shoes, Liz. We'll be back after lunch."

Finally I turned them over. Maybe she was hoping for a mini-earthquake that would flatten the shoe department. I just knew it was going to be a bumpy lunch. She would change the subject completely, get me involved in a totally different conversation, and then as we were leaving, wham! start the pressure again about the proper shoes.

"Where should we go?" I asked.

"Gram is going to meet us in the restaurant on top of Bloomie's, remember?"

Good, I thought. Mom will try to get Gram to act as referee, though usually Gram tries to stay out of any disagreement the two of us are having.

She was kind of unique, Gram was. She was a real homebody—had raised three kids, been president of the P.T.A., and was the first person people called when they wanted action in her home town. She sat on the Board of Education, which was an elected position, still knitted all her own sweaters, and always had freshly baked cookies. Of course Mom thought she was old fashioned. "With your talents," she once told her, "you could be making an extraordinary salary. Why give your services away with all this volunteer work?"

"Because I'm good at it and it makes me feel good,"

answered Gram, "and I get satisfaction I could never get from a paycheck."

Gram was waiting at the head of the line in the restaurant. She took one look at our faces and said, "Uh-oh, I see storm clouds ahead."

I kissed her hello but glared back at Mom. "Why do we have to eat here? Can't we just have a hot dog at Snacktime, out in the mall?"

"You have to stand at Snacktime, Liz. I want to slip my shoes off for a few minutes. And speaking of shoes," Mom turned to Gram, "you are never going to believe the shoes your granddaughter wants for Larry's wedding."

I turned my back and studied the menu posted on the wall. Finally the hostess seated us.

Mom patted my hand. "See, they have a chef's salad or a turkey sandwich."

I was determined to be obstinate. "You know I just like a quick hamburger or something when we're shopping."

"All right, let's see. Hamburgers. Oh, here's one. Hamburger diet delight."

I knew I was acting like a complete baby, but I had Mom on the run trying to smooth things out so we would have a calm lunch. I realized that Grandma would feel uncomfortable with all this bickering, but I couldn't stop myself. Maybe Mom could tell me what to wear, but she wasn't going to tell me what to put in my stomach.

"Gross," I said. "A hamburger on a plate with a clump of cottage cheese and sliced pineapple. I hate cottage cheese and I hate pineapple, and you're always telling me I'm too thin."

Gram put the menu down. "I promised Grandpa I'd meet him in the tool department of Sears after lunch, but if you two are going to carry on like this, I think I'll leave right now."

"Don't be silly, Mama, sit still. Liz is just having one of her days."

I liked that. *I* was having one of my days. What about *her?*

Mom signaled the waitress. "I'll have a junior chef's salad." She glanced at Gram, who nodded acquiescence, and they both looked at me. "My daughter would like a hamburger, but without the cottage cheese and pineapple."

The pencil stopped in midair. "Sorry, no substitutions. See? Right there on the bottom of the menu. No substitutions."

"That's all right." Mom had her negotiating voice on. "We just want the hamburger on a roll, without all the other things."

"We don't have a hamburger roll."

I continued my childish behavior by sitting back and folding my arms across my chest in my I-told-you-but-you-wouldn't-listen posture.

Mom forced a smile and tried again. "What kind of rolls do you have?" She asked the waitress.

"Well," the waitress said, "I guess we could put the hamburger on an English muffin."

"I hate English muffins." I cringed inwardly at how whiney I sounded. In another minute I'd be sucking my thumb.

Mom was ready to explode but took a breath instead. To the waitress she explained, "Put the burger on an English muffin and hold the cottage cheese and pineapple." She held up her hand in anticipation. "Don't worry, I'll pay for the whole plate."

Gram spoke up and covered my hands with hers. "Enough already, Liz. You're sixteen and you're acting as if you're six."

That hurt, even though I knew she was right. Still, I felt the tears forming behind my lids. I suddenly wished I was a little girl again, when Gram always seemed to take my side against Mom's pushiness, as she called it.

"It looks as if I'll have to be the mediator. Now what's been happening with the two of you this morning?" Gram asked.

"You won't believe it, Mama, but wait, I want to take a couple of aspirins."

We watched Mom gulp down the two little white pills, rubbing the back of her neck at the same time.

"I could use a couple of aspirins, too." If Mom was insinuating that I had given her a pain in the neck, well, the feeling was mutual.

"Hey, time out, time out." Gram made a little T with her hands, the way umpires do in a football game. "Now one of you speak at a time and tell me why you're both in such a state when you were looking forward to this shopping trip."

Mom began. "Your granddaughter has absolutely no taste or style of her own. All I've heard this morning is about the things her friends wear and how much like them she wants to be. She has absolutely no individuality about herself."

"Why? Because I don't want to wear pleated skirts? What makes you think that's so stylish?"

Gram made the T sign again because our lunch had arrived. As we were eating she asked Mom, "Now tell me about the shoes."

Mom did, graphically. My face flushed as she carried on.

"And on top of the fact that they are cheap looking, ugly, and tacky, she'll probably break her ankle before we even leave the house."

We were interrupted then by a chorus of hellos. It was Mary Jo, Donna, and a couple of my other friends. They all knew Mom and Gram and had seen us from across the floor. I had told them I'd be in the mall today with Mom.

Donna and Mary Jo spotted my packages and leaned over to see what I had bought. It gave me a minute to study them. We all wore our hair loose and long. I was wearing sneakers, but the others had their Hush Puppies on. I had almost worn mine, but my sneakers were more comfortable for shopping. We all had blue quilted down ski jackets and jeans and collared shirts underneath our long-sleeve crew neck sweaters.

It felt good to have them around me, as if I was safe and didn't stick out oddly in the adult world surrounding us.

They left after a few minutes, Gram watching them go, a faint smile on her lips.

"See what I mean, Liz?" said Mom. "You're all sweet, great-looking girls, but you dress so much alike that you're practically interchangeable. You each need a style of your own. Well, I have to make a telephone call." Mom glanced at her watch and threw some bills down on the table. "I'll meet you both in the shoe department in twenty minutes, okay?"

Gram started to protest. "I have to meet your father."

"Mama, couldn't you spend fifteen minutes in the shoe department to see these beauties?"

Gram followed Mom across the room with her eyes. She still had that faint smile on her lips.

I watched Mom go, too. You could see heads turn as she

walked past. It wasn't just her clothes and the way she was put together; it was her confidence, her air of being someone. My friends and I still liked to walk in a group with shoulders touching. I don't know why. I guess it gives us a feeling of security.

"Nylon blouses."

"What did you say, Gram?"

"Nylon blouses. I'd almost forgotten. They all wore nylon blouses, as sheer as lace curtains. Underneath they had embroidered slips or camisoles covering up their bras. And of course they had little balls of cotton inserted into the tips of the padded bras to give them that pointed look. How we used to fight about that!"

"Who? You and Mom? Mom used to fill out her bras with cotton?"

"Your mother would have filled them out with silver bullets if that had been what her friends were doing. And they used to dip the cotton balls in perfume before they left home in order to smell sexy. Everyone reeked from evaporated Evening in Paris."

"Did they wear those icky full skirts, too?" I leaned closer to Gram.

"Oh yes. They had full taffeta or felt skirts and wore rough horse-hair crinoline petticoats that could stand by themselves. And of course an elastic cinch belt held everything together."

I took another sip of Tab. "What else, Gram?" I was fascinated at the picture of my mother dressing like her girlfriends, in the uniform of the day.

"The only thing I fought your mom over was the ballerinas."

"Ballerinas?"

"Yes. Real ballet slippers were 'in.' The kids used to wear them for street shoes, and of course after two wearings on concrete, the soles were completely gone. They were just simple black flats tied at the front with a tiny black cord. Everyone wore them except your mother."

"Why not?"

"Because I wouldn't buy them for her. I didn't believe in them. They were absolutely not for everyday use. No support for arches or ankles."

"What did Mom do?"

"After she told me I was ruining her life and making her look like a freak?"

"Mom said that?" I giggled. Mom afraid her life was going to be ruined over a pair of shoes?

"There was some kind of a junior dance—they were always having dances in the fifties. And your Mom left the house with her friends in a pair of solidly built flat suede shoes."

"What happened?"

"Most of it Grandpa and I pieced together later, but about 10:30 we got a call from Overlook Hospital that your mom was there with a broken ankle."

"I don't believe it. From the shoes you bought her?"

"No, it seems that when she got to the dance she borrowed a pair of ballerinas from one of her friends and hid her navy flats in the girls' room." Gram asked the waitress to refill her coffee cup. "I wonder if those shoes are still under some sink in that school."

"Go on, Gram. What happened next?"

"Well, I guess the ballerinas were old and a little too big for her, and one of the soft soles was coming loose. It happened during the bunny-hop. You've probably seen them do it on TV. The rhythm of the dance is simple. You hold the waist of the person in front of you and weave and hop to the music: right foot, right foot, left foot, left, front, back, hop, hop, hop. It must have happened on one of the hops. The right ballerina caught on the heel of the girl in line in front of her. It wasn't a simple fall. She tore the ligaments in her right ankle and fractured the bone."

"I'll bet you were ready to kill her when you got to the hospital."

"Not exactly. To tell you the truth, I was so glad that she was alive and well and that it was just a broken ankle, I never said a word."

"What did you do to her?"

"Do?"

"I mean, was she grounded or did you take away her allowance or anything like that?"

Gram drew a square on the tablecloth with the tines of her fork. "I guess we figured the broken ankle was kind of punishment enough. When I walked into the emergency room the nurse said to me, 'Your daughter's things are on that table if you want to take them home.' I thought she must be mistaken because there were these old, dilapidated ballerinas right on top of the pile. I remember I turned to your mom. She was in a lot of pain, and they had just given her a shot so they could set the ankle." Gram laughed. "Darn if she didn't sit straight up in bed and stare me right down. 'Go ahead,' she said. 'Aren't you going to gloat and tell me how right you were and how stupid it was for me to wear the shoes?' "

"And did you?" What a great story! I'd love to have heard Gram really give it to Mom for lying, for sneaking around and switching shoes when she shouldn't have.

Gram put the fork down and took my two hands in hers. "No, we never spoke about it again."

"Did Mom ever wear ballerinas again?"

"As a matter of fact, after her ankle healed I went out and bought her a pair. The girls were still wearing them. I don't think she ever did wear them, though."

I shook my head. "It's hard to picture Mom being so caught up in a fad that she'd do something like that, and I'm surprised you didn't really use the opportunity to sock it to her, Gram."

"It wouldn't have done any good. And besides, your Mom, just like you, was almost through with—well, I guess it's a special growing up time in the life of a young woman when she feels she's got to be like everybody else, before she's developed her own taste and set of rules. I guess you could say it's a very special brief season. You just have to pass through it on the way to growing up. And now we'd better get going, because your Mom will have our heads. Come on, I'm anxious to see these fantastic shoes of yours."

Mom was in the shoe department. Only the slow staccato tapping of her right foot indicated that she was annoyed at being kept waiting.

The two boxes were side by side. I tried a pump on my right foot and the high heeled sandal on my left.

"Well, what do you think?" I turned to Grandma.

"I think that you should take whatever you feel you'll be most comfortable in."

"No, Mama, that's a cop-out," said Mom. "Which do you think looks better on her?"

"I repeat myself: the pair that she feels best in."

I walked back and forth. The sandals were killing my

feet; I wouldn't be able to last two dances in them. But if I gave in, my mother would be so smug about the whole thing. No, I couldn't do that. But Mom was right; the gold were tacky looking and would spoil the outfit.

There was a sudden influx of energy as my girlfriends walked into the department. "There she is." They surrounded me. "Oh, let's see, Liz. Walk a little."

I watched their faces as they studied my feet and I also watched Mom and Grandma watching their faces.

"So, girls, what do you think?"

Mary Jo spoke for all of them. "The gold are super. They make your legs look so sexy."

Donna continued, "Oh, definitely. The gold are to die for. My mother would never let me wear them, but they're super shoes."

My heart fell, and my little toe was pinching like crazy. To tell the truth, I had been hoping that my friends would pick the plain pumps. Dyed to match, they'd be spectacular with the dress. It was babyish to reject an idea just because it came from my mother. Besides, now that I knew she had been just as insecure about her looks and style when she was my age, I guess I could accept her opinion.

My friends were still oohing and aahing over the sandals. If it was up to me, I would have taken the plain ones. But how could I disappoint them? They were all excited and had agreed on the gold. I guess they were still caught in the middle of that very brief season, but something told me, as I handed the box to the salesman, that I was almost ready to pass right through.

Trophy

STACEY MICHAELS WAS TRYING to pin up a notice on the school's trophy showcase. "Literary Magazine. Calling all poets, writers, photographers, illustrators— *The Spectrum* needs you!"

"Need help?" Rob Abrams didn't wait for an answer. He reached over Stacey's head for a thumbtack, took the notice out of her hands, and deftly pinned it in a prominent position.

"Thanks," she said. She wobbled a little on her clogs, and Rob put out a hand to steady her. "Thanks twice," she said. "Do you write?" She pointed to the notice.

"No, I play." He pointed to the showcase, to a large silver cup on which was engraved NEW JERSEY STATE SOCCER CHAMPS, followed by a list of high schools. Brownfield High was the last name on the list. "Soccer. I'm Number 21."

No answer from Stacy as she gathered her papers together.

"Captain of last year's state championship team. Soon to be the first team to be champs two years in a row."

"I really don't follow sports too much."

"I'm Rob Abrams." Rob was usually recognized by every member of the student body, even girls who didn't follow sports.

"Well, hi." Stacey started off down the hall.

"Hey, wait up." Rob grabbed his notebook from the showcase and caught up with her. "I don't remember seeing you around. Who do you hang out with?"

Stacey looked with dark brown eyes that were shaded with eyelashes so long they tangled at the corners of her eyes. "Hang out? I don't hang out with anybody. My name is Stacey Michaels, and I just transferred here."

"From where?"

"You name it. My mother's a pharmaceutical engineer, and I've been in five schools in the past three years."

"Your mother?"

Stacey was used to people's being surprised at her mother's occupation. Actually her father was an engineer, too, but Stacey hadn't seen him since she was eleven. Six years ago. He had left to build bridges and dams in exotic lands, and all Stacey had was a collection of unusual postcards and miniature dolls that he sent from each stop.

Her mother stayed with one of the largest pharmaceutical companies in the country. Dr. Michaels was a trouble-shooter who traveled from plant to plant to straighten out problems.

"If you don't hang out with anyone, how about meeting me this afternoon? Around five? I'll take you home."

"Around five?"

"Yeah, well, I've got soccer practice right after school. I finish about five."

"What am I supposed to do while you're practicing?" Stacey continued down the hall. She swung her chestnut-colored hair over her shoulders, and Rob caught a fragrance so faintly sweet that he almost thought he had imagined it.

Most of the girls Rob knew would be happy to wait until he finished practice. Obviously Stacey was not going to be one of them.

"Hey, don't get mad. I just thought maybe you were staying anyway for the magazine."

"No, I just hung the notice for them. I do my writing at home."

"Do you have to walk so fast?"

"You're a soccer player. Keep up."

"What if I call you?"

"What if?" Stacey turned the corner.

Rob yelled out, "Your phone number?"

She stopped a moment, tore off a piece of notebook paper, scrawled something on it, and handed it to him without looking.

And so it began. Slowly at first. Stacey was very cautious. She was too used to moving on from place to place. She went to her first soccer game. The team was fantastic. They were sure to be state champs for the second year in a row. Stacey found herself yelling with the rest of the student body. College scouts showed up to talk to some of the outstanding players, Rob among them.

Stacey made friends slowly among the other students, but there wasn't anybody she felt especially close to. Except Rob. He was the first one who visited the apartment she shared with her mother. It looked as if they had just moved in, even though they had been in town six weeks. Dr. Michaels had promised that they would stay there long enough for Stacey to graduate, even if her work at the plant finished early.

There were cartons of books in the corner of the living room. Shades were up, but no draperies. Stacey showed Rob her room. It was the only room that looked finished, since Stacey had done everything herself. Her high-rise bed was draped with a corduroy cover, and lots of throw pillows made it more of a couch than a bed. She had a large, floppy beanbag chair, a desk and a dresser, and posters covered walls that hadn't been painted yet. She didn't have rock stars on her walls. Her posters were of oceans, mountains, broad horizons depicting the five continents.

Rob walked over to the bookcase. On the top shelf her miniature doll collection was lined up. He reached for one.

"No. Please don't touch, Rob."

"I'm sorry. I just wanted to see where it was from." He stuck his hands in his pockets and toed the shag throw rug.

Stacey smoothed the costumed skirt of the doll. "Jakarta. My dad was there four years ago."

"You mean you haven't even seen him once in all these years?" Rob pointed at the silent dolls that stared solemnly back out of porcelain faces.

"He jumps from one job right to another."

"How come you and your mother didn't go with him?"

Stacey got busy with some record albums. "After graduation this summer, I'm going to meet him in Paris. He promised. And I don't know why I'm telling you all this. How would you feel if I asked personal questions about your family?"

Rob turned her around and smoothed a cheek with one hand.

"Hey, Stace. I'm sorry. It just seems funny. I mean, are they divorced or something?"

"No. It's just that my mother is based in the States, and his job means travel. They have an open marriage. No one gets in anyone's way as far as careers go."

Rob looked as if he had another question, but the fragrance from Stacey's hair got to him, and he kissed her instead.

The Saturday before Thanksgiving Stacey waited for the soccer game to begin. She hugged herself and zipped her windbreaker closed to the neck. It was really getting cold. She watched the team warm up. They must be freezing in those shorts and high socks, though Rob said they were never cold once they started to run up and down the field, at least—not if they were doing their jobs right.

The game went off as scheduled, and Brownfield took the lead with an early goal. Lois Frieden, who dated the goalie, shivered and stamped her feet on the bleachers. "It's freezing. I hope they hurry and win this championship before they have to play in snow."

Stacey agreed.

"Hey, Stacey, maybe you and Rob would like to chip in for a team party at the end of the season?"

Stacey hugged herself tighter. "Rob and I? Rob can do whatever he wants, but I have nothing to do with the team."

"I just thought since you've been going together, maybe you'd like to help plan it."

"No. If Rob wants me to go, I will. But otherwise I don't care." Stacey turned back to the field. She didn't seem to notice Lois nudge the girl next to her and mouth the word "snob" while pointing to Stacey.

Brownfield was ahead. One of the forwards had the ball and was working it toward the opposition goal. There was a shout from the crowd: "Player down. Player down." Stacey looked back to the other end of the field. The coach and team doctor were running over to a crumpled player. Play didn't stop, so most people weren't aware of the injury.

It was Rob. The two men half walked, half dragged him off the field while the cheerleaders gave him an individual cheer. Stacey left the game, not caring about the final score.

She waited at home for Rob's call.

"Hi, Stace."

"Are you all right, Rob?"

"Just a bad shot to my thigh. Listen, can you come over?"

Stacey didn't answer.

"I'm going to be kind of laid up all weekend." Rob was understating his condition. He was wrapped in ice from his knee to his thigh, and his leg was elevated on pillows. The team doctor had told him to stay in that position for 48 hours to make sure the swelling on the leg went down.

Stacey traced a square outline on the wall where a picture had been removed by the previous tenant. Stacey and her mother never lived in a place long enough for walls to fade around pictures.

"Mom finally got a painter to come in here this weekend, and she promised to stay home and get the apartment set. I've got to be here so she won't run off to the plant."

Before Rob could protest, Stacey finished with, "You rest up and I'll catch you on Monday." She'd have to remember to tell him the painter got sick and couldn't make it; otherwise, the next time he came over, he'd wonder why the walls still weren't done.

When Stacey saw him Monday morning, Rob was on crutches. He was cool to her at first, but when she smiled and offered to carry his books he warmed up.

There were two weeks left until the state finals. The doctor was doubtful about whether Rob could play. He was stretched out on Stacey's bed while she typed a term paper.

"What if we lose the finals because I don't play?"

She answered without losing her typing rhythm. "You mean you're going to make the whole difference to the team?"

"You can make me feel like a conceited idiot. Remember, most of the plays are made around me."

"So then play."

"The doctor says I can permanently injure myself. Something called myositis ossificans."

"What's that?"

"I don't know exactly. Something like permanent calcium deposits forming in the bad leg if I don't let it rest completely. I'd have to be off sports for about a year. No track in the spring."

"What if you just play the last game—for the championship—and worry about the spring later?"

"I don't know. The doctor kind of scared me. I don't want to be limping the rest of my life because of a high school game."

She turned back to the typewriter. "I'm sure you'll make the right decision."

Rob put his hand on the back of her neck and rubbed. "Rob, please. I've got to finish this paper."

"Go ahead, keep typing." He reached over and kissed her cheek. "It's not only the team, you know. I could get a scholarship if I'm not injured. And I'd kind of like you to see me finish in a blaze of glory." He looked up at the watching dolls, then leaned toward her again.

Stacey pushed the carriage return on the typewriter, turned her chair around, and let herself drift into Rob's arms. "How can I concentrate when you're kissing me like that?"

After a few minutes he murmured into her hair, "Stace?"

"Yes."

"I'll play. I'll be careful, and it is the state cup."

Rob reported back to the team. Stacey watched him at

practice. His leg was wrapped in ace bandages from knee to thigh, and he wore a brace over that. Maybe his timing was a bit wrong, but it was only when he was off the field that she noticed his face grimacing with pain.

The day of the finals, it rained. The field was loaded with mud and gigantic puddles—dangerous enough when players were in top condition but deadly when they weren't completely up to par.

The first quarter was uneventful: no score for either side. Most of the spectators left. The rain was heavy, and it was too uncomfortable sitting out in the open bleachers. Stacey huddled under her slicker. She had two pairs of socks on but was soaked through to the skin.

In the last quarter their team broke through with a goal. Rob didn't score but he ran the ball up the field and passed to the wing, who looped it over the opposition goalie.

Stacey couldn't wait to get home into dry clothes. The phone was ringing as she toweled off.

"Why didn't you wait for me after the game?"

"Oh Rob, I was soaked. Besides, you had to go with the team."

"I know, but I looked all over for you. Lois waited for Jerry." There was quiet from Stacey's end of the phone.

"How many times do I have to tell you that I don't care what other people do?"

"Okay, but listen. I have something for you."

"Rob, I don't want you spending money on me."

"It's nothing that cost money. It's something special I want you to have. Can I come over later?"

Dr. Michaels' secretary had already called. Stacy's mother wouldn't be home for dinner. She should take something out of the freezer.

"You can't stay late. I've got a physics quiz tomorrow."

Rob was over within the hour. He was back on crutches, a little pale, but he had a big smile on his face.

Stacey pointed to the crutches. "I didn't see you fall."

"The leg swelled. I can't bend my knee. No weight bearing, and it looks like no track."

"Maybe you shouldn't have played. I didn't tell you to."

"I know. It was my decision. Anyway, we're state champs —second year in a row. Look what the coach had ready and all made up for us. He was so sure." He handed her a miniature trophy, an exact copy of the large one that stood in the glass showcase at the school. It read, "Brownfield High Soccer Champs. Rob Abrams, Center Forward."

"I want you to have it, Stace."

She handed it back. "Oh no. It's yours. You worked hard for it—too hard maybe." She tapped one of the crutches.

"Please, Stace. I want you to have it. It'll mean more to me if I think of its being here with you."

She threw her arms around his neck. "You're really sweet. You know that, Rob Abrams?"

After Rob had left, Stacey took out a soft linen handkerchief and rubbed the trophy carefully. Then she opened her top drawer. In the corner was a small stack of postcards tied with a blue ribbon. From Asia, Africa, and Australia. The messages were so similar they could have been mimeographed. "Hi, sweetheart. The job is going to take longer than I expected. You should be receiving a package from me soon. Say hello to Mom for me. Love, Daddy." The last one was dated nine months ago.

In the front of the drawer there were some small objects. A Phi Beta Kappa key from the boy in Illinois who hadn't known she was a high school junior. A football charm from the captain of the football team in Tallahassee. Stacey placed the soccer trophy next to the class ring of the editor of the school paper in Michigan. Then she closed the drawer.

She changed her pattern of walking to class the next day. Rob finally caught up with her in the cafeteria. "Where have you been?" He was puffing from the crutches. "I've been looking all over for you this morning."

"Oh Rob, I'm late. I don't even have time to talk. I'm doing an extra-credit project for history." And off she went down the hall.

He called her every day for a week. She was always busy. Friday morning he was stationed by her locker. "Okay, Stacey, what gives with you anyway?"

"Nothing, Rob. Just nothing."

"Why the deep freeze? What did I do?"

"Nothing. It's just that I don't want to get hung up with one person, that's all."

"That's what you call it? Being hung up?"

"You know what I mean. Can't we just be friends?"

He shifted his crutches. "Sure. Friends. Well, right now, Stacey, I've got a whole stack of friends. So I don't think I can really use any more. You won't mind if I pass on the friend bit."

"Suit yourself." And she slammed the locker door. Rob limped off down the hall shaking his head from side to side.

When Stacey left school that afternoon she passed through the front hall. There was a crowd around the glass showcase. The top shelf was empty except for a sign that read, "This spot reserved for the Brownfield High School Basketball Cup!" The soccer trophy had been moved to the bottom shelf. It was off to the side, and the silver looked as if it were beginning to tarnish.

To Francie,
with Love

*I*T SEEMED AS IF we had just had Thanksgiving turkey, and now Mom was getting out the Christmas tree decorations. But then, she had to get an early start. She worked full time as a bookkeeper in Dalton's department store.

"Francie, please move some of these college catalogs. I need room."

"I will, Mom." They were spread over the kitchen, piled up on my desk, and stacked on the coffee table. Senior year was decision time, time to plan the future.

I picked them up, and Mom filled the empty space with a box of Christmas lights.

"We'd better test these." She said that every year. They always worked because she and Dad went to the after-Christmas sales and restocked on bulbs and decorations. Even the holiday cards she was addressing were bought last year. Fresh and unused, but still last year's.

I flipped through the catalogs. I loved the smell, the feel, of the shiny paper and the shadowy images of college life. Catalogs were probably the closest I'd get to that mythical campus life.

My father was a carpenter, and though he worked long hours and took odd jobs on weekends, we had a tough time financially. Mom had been thirty-eight when I was born. They always seemed old to me and very quiet, more like grandparents than parents. I think they were just worn out from working so hard.

I had a lot of trouble getting them to allow me freedom, and of course they were very nervous about my relationship with my boyfriend, Bruce Greene.

I hadn't seen Bruce since he left for college in September. I wrote, and he phoned, but Christmas would be our first reunion. I couldn't wait. It would mean missing some work. I was a part-time cashier at the supermarket, and every penny went into the bank for school. I still wouldn't be able to afford dormitory costs and travel expenses to one of the "catalog schools," but my guidance counselor told me I could count on a scholarship to the state university. I'd live at home and be able to keep my supermarket job. Of course I wouldn't be surrounded by ivy-covered buildings. State U. had grown up haphazardly, with buildings tucked away among delicatessens, laundries, and apartment buildings.

I wanted to study architecture, to design homes: soaring, open-spaced houses nestled in wooded lots open to sun and air, with freedom to move. My drafting teacher said I had real aptitude.

"Francie, your father and I are going to pick out the tree tonight. Would you like to go with us?"

I had been doodling—a high cathedral ceiling with a greenhouse roof to capture light. Our four-room apartment was dark and crowded. Mom meant well, but there was just never any privacy. Dreams were cut off too quickly. Maybe that's why it seemed as if my parents never had any.

Mom had pulled out her little metal shopping cart. "I need a couple of things from the market." She looked exceptionally tired as she glanced out the window. It had started to snow.

"Let me go with you. I know where all the specials are."

The market was full of holiday shoppers. As I squeezed our cart through the crowded aisles, I noticed Bruce's mother just a few feet away, carefully examining the produce. "There's Leslie," I said.

Mom sighed. "I can't understand how you can call Mrs. Greene by her first name. It just doesn't seem respectful."

"Oh Mom, she insists. Anyway, she's more like Bruce's sister than his mother."

Bruce's family was just the opposite of mine. His parents were young, and he had a younger brother and sister. They lived in a rambling ranch-style house filled with expensive furniture and lush carpets.

"Francie. Hi!" Mrs. Greene pushed her basket over to us. "And, Mrs. Slabin, how are you?" Even her voice was young. She was wearing a velour warm-up suit under her fun fur. I knew it was her daytime fun fur because I had seen the sleek dark mink she wore for evening.

"Well, this is it, Francie. Senior year." She turned to Mother. "Isn't it exciting, Mrs. Slabin? Looking through catalogs and deciding on schools?"

"How're the kids, Mrs. Greene? I mean, Leslie," I said, trying to change the subject. Bruce's family had studied the catalogs together. It was a game to them. Mom and Dad never said anything about my catalogs—or about colleges either.

"Oh Francie." Mrs. Greene slapped the edge of the basket. "I don't know if he's called you yet . . . but I'm afraid Bruce won't be home for Christmas." She went on, "Dan and I decided to take the kids to St. Thomas. Bruce doesn't want to go, so he's going skiing in Vermont. You know how he is about snow."

Her words felt like a delayed punch, but I don't think

I showed it, and finally, after some more idle chatter, she waved and continued down the aisle.

I didn't even notice what Mom had put in the cart. As she went to check out, I told her I'd be right back. I went to the office and told the supervisor that I'd be available to work straight through Christmas vacation: time and a half for working the holiday when all I had wanted was to spend it with Bruce.

The snow had settled, covering everything with that special clean look. Mom wanted to pick up Dad's shoes from the shoemaker, but I sent her home and promised to make the stop myself. I found a park bench and sat for a moment, catching a stray snowflake on the tip of my tongue, feeling the wet coldness melt. It wouldn't be long before cars and people would turn the white into a dirty slush. Snow for Christmas—under our tree, in the city streets, and up in Vermont. I shivered and, after catching another snowflake, moved on to finish my errand.

The phone in our kitchen was ringing when I got back. "I'll get it," I said to Mom, who was still unpacking groceries.

It was Bruce.

"You sound all out of breath. Been jogging or ice-skating?"

"Neither—I just came back from the market."

"I miss you."

"Oh Bruce." Just his voice could start my heart fluttering. I tried to stretch the phone cord as far as I could to have some privacy. I managed to make it to the hallway between the two bedrooms.

I told Bruce that I had met his mother. He didn't wait for me to continue.

"Did she tell you? I feel crummy about not being home for Christmas. But they'll be away, and the snow is the thickest it's been in Vermont."

I guess I was too quiet. "Francie? You're not mad, are you? Even though I'll miss Christmas, I'll be home the day after New Year's, and we'll still have a week before I go back to school."

I couldn't think of anything to say. He had already made the decision.

"Francie? Do you think your mom and dad would let you come up to Vermont? It's a public ski lodge. We'd be well chaperoned. I'll rent skis for you, and you can borrow my sister's ski clothes."

It was his way of telling me that he wanted to be with me. He knew I didn't have the money to go skiing. At least my rival was a curving trail of snow and not a curvy co-ed.

The next couple of weeks, I worked extra hours at the market and helped Mom at home. She made lots of baked goods. We wrapped them in cellophane and trimmed them with ribbons and candy canes. One night we were wrapping an exceptionally nice fruitcake with dried pineapple rings circled across the top. I don't know if it was the heat from the oven or if she was blushing, but Mom pointed to it and said, "I thought . . . that is, maybe you would want to give this one to Bruce's mother and father."

That was a lot from her: acknowledging my relationship with Bruce and sealing it with the tradition of a fruitcake.

The day before, a package had arrived for me from Dalton's: a designer scarf with a beautiful pattern of soft, blurry flowers that reminded me of Monet's "Water Lilies." "To Francie, with love, from all the Greenes."

Dad couldn't understand why the designer's big initials were in the corner. "Those aren't yours. Why would you wear something with another person's initials on it?"

I tried to explain about status symbols and how the initials told everyone that you could afford this designer's work. Mother listened quietly and said, "It's like when you finish a piece of furniture and put your initials and the date on it."

Dad laughed. "I'd carve them five feet high if someone would pay me extra."

We had the tradition of opening our presents on Christmas Eve, mostly because we gave each other practical gifts that we used on Christmas Day. We'd give Dad new tools or a warm sweater for work, and Mom might receive a new roaster that she could cook Christmas dinner in.

Even when I was little, Mom would tell me that Santa didn't have money for lots of toys and clothes, so we'd figure out what I really needed: a new scarf, mittens, a three-ring notebook, a winter jacket that we bought on sale a couple of weeks before (so we wouldn't tire Santa out), and if there was any money left, I'd ask Santa for a Snoopy doll. Christmas Eve my packages would be under the tree, marked, "To Francie, with love."

But I was working this Christmas Eve. Mom and Dad said they'd wait up for me so we could open our presents as usual. This year I had asked for something special. I told Mom to ask everyone in the family that we exchanged presents with to pool all the gift money, add it to Mom and Dad's, and get me a typewriter. I need one for college. They were expensive, but I cut out ads that showed Christmas specials. Mom had taken them and said, "We'll see."

I had bought Mom a special pocketbook. It felt like butter, and the swirls and pigmentation of the leather constantly changed from gold to deep caramel. She allowed herself only two bags, black for winter and white for summer. "They go with everything," she'd say.

For Daddy I had a pair of fur-lined gloves. His hands were always torn up from work. Mom had to rub them with cream at night. They would crack open from the cold, especially the calluses on his palms.

It was crazy in the store on Christmas Eve. My feet were killing me. The store manager had asked us to dress for the holidays, and I was wearing a pair of platform shoes. It began to feel as if the evening would go on forever, filled with housewives who had forgotten bread crumbs for the turkey stuffing and rushing men trying to replace burned-out Christmas bulbs. Bruce would be coming in from the slopes now. I could picture the scene: après-ski, girls in beautiful lounging clothes, a large roaring fire, and everyone sitting around toasting marshmallows—and each other.

I felt a tap on the shoulder. It was Jill Fried. "Go home, Francie Slabin. I'm here to relieve you."

"What do you mean?"

Jill got very busy straightening the grocery bags so I wouldn't see her blush. "In the ecumenical spirit I decided that you should be home enjoying your holiday."

"Jill, that's terrific of you."

She held her hand up. "No thanks, please. Don't worry, there are lots of Jewish holidays coming up, so I expect to be paid back."

I had my jacket on in two seconds. "Just let me know, and I'll be here."

Mom and Dad were putting packages under the tree. They were surprised to see me so early.

"Did you eat?" Mom asked.

"I had a hamburger around five."

Dad was fussing with the timer for the lights. The tree looked pretty, solid, and unchanged. It had looked like this when I was seven and would probably be the same when I was thirty-seven. Each year the Greenes had something different and spectacular. This year Leslie had said they were having a silver tree with all silver trimmings.

I turned out the overhead light, and the reds and greens blinked on and off, throwing soft shadows on the crèche below the tree branches.

"Shall we open our gifts now?" Dad asked.

"Gee, it's only seven. What will we do for the rest of the night?" I asked.

"I agree with Dad. Let's open our presents now, and then you can help me make some Jell-O molds for tomorrow."

Mom and Dad had never been so anxious to open presents before. They must have gotten me the typewriter and wanted to see if I liked it. That would be great.

I gave Mother her gift; she didn't open it. Dad didn't open his either. Instead, they handed me a long narrow box. I was puzzled. This obviously was not a typewriter. It was beautifully wrapped and had a tiny Christmas tag with a bright wreath in the corner: "To Francie, with love. Your mother and father."

I untied it slowly. They were watching every move. I tried to make a joke. "Now, when I lift the lid, is something going to pop out at me?" No one laughed. I opened the top and pushed aside the tissue paper. It looked like a wallet. My heart fell. What was so special about a wallet? No, it wasn't a wallet. It was a little book. A passbook, small, blue leather with the words First National Bank on the cover. I opened it. There were pages and pages of black letters with dates and figures entered on it. I didn't understand. I looked up, and Mom pointed to the front page. It read: "A special Christmas Club in trust for Francie Slabin, opened Christmas 1967, to be redeemed Christmas 1984, held by Frederick and Margaret Slabin."

I had been born in September 1967. Mother and Dad had opened it the year of my birth. Every single month had a sum of money entered, from my birth until December of this, my seventeenth, year.

Dad took Mother's hand. "It's for your college, Francie, for those beautiful schools you've been thinking about. We've seen you studying the pictures in the catalogs."

"You were just a tiny baby, but we knew you'd want to do great things." Mother was smoothing one of the calluses on Dad's palm.

"We wanted to be ready. Now you can pick any school you want, even if it means you'll be far away from us." They were talking in unison. I studied the entries. They had never missed. Some of the entries for 1978 were small. That was the year Dad had pneumonia. That same year everyone in the family had chipped in to help Grandma Slabin with her mortgage payments. In 1979 there were double sums. I remember Dad had had a special job helping Mr. Saunders build an addition to his house. And Mother had taken only one vacation week. Entry after entry. All the trips they never took, the new furniture, the fun fur, and special treats that were never bought. It was overwhelming. I could actually count my mother's overtime hours and the blisters on my father's hands with this passbook.

I had to leave the room. I ran into the bathroom and

turned on the faucet full strength so they wouldn't hear me cry.

"Is she all right?" I heard Dad ask.

"She's fine. She'll be right back." How could I have been so arrogant about my dreams and desires as not to realize that they had some too? Life wasn't just vacations and silver Christmas trees and spacious ranch houses. I thought of those shiny catalogs. My parents had given me freedom to choose what I really wanted to do. But hadn't they always? How would I have dared to dream of being an architect, if they hadn't always given me confidence in myself? And actually, did it really matter where I studied as long as I worked to make that dream come true? Now that I was able to picture myself walking along a tree-lined campus, it no longer seemed all that important.

The phone rang. "Francie," Mother called, "it's Bruce."

I ran into the kitchen. She handed me the phone. "I'll go. You can talk alone."

"No, don't go, Mom." I grabbed her hand and held it. "I'll only be a minute."

"Hi, Bruce." I tried to smooth the veins in her hand while I waited to hear his familiar voice.

"Oh, Francie, I miss you. This place is crowded with families, but it just doesn't seem like Christmas."

He talked on for a few minutes about the snow conditions. Finally he said, "I love you, and don't forget I'll be home next week. I'd leave now, but I paid for everything in advance."

"That's okay, Bruce." Dad had walked into the kitchen. He took Mother's other hand, and we stood grinning at each other. I was attached to the phone and to Mother, and he moved toward me to complete the circle. It seemed very important for us all to be touching. "Mom and Dad and I need some time alone this week anyway. We have to make a lot of decisions about college."

"Say hello to them for me, and wish them a Merry Christmas."

"I will, Bruce."

"Oh Francie? Did your father hang those long icicles on the tree like he did last year?"

"Yes, and he'll hang them the same way next year."

"I was thinking about them this afternoon. You won't take the tree down before next week, will you? Because right now I feel as if Christmas passed me by."

"It'll be up, Bruce. But don't worry, even if it wasn't, it's been Christmas in this house for seventeen years."

The
Moon Cookies

*M*ARCY STUCK HER TONGUE OUT at the mirror. Blah! That's what it was, she had the blahs. What's worse, she had a pimple—right in the middle of her chin. She reached for the blemish coverup, dabbed some on, and tried to blend it in. No use. Tawny Rachel just didn't do the job on her fair skin. She couldn't decide which was more noticeable, the pimple or the make-up streaks.

"Marcy, hurry up. You'll miss the bus again." That was Mom. She sounded almost cheerful this morning. Actually, Mom hadn't been too cheerful since Grandma Martin had come to visit. Well, it was supposed to be a visit—that was three months ago. Marcy reached for her hair blower.

"Marcy." The voice was persistent.

"Okay, Mom, I'm coming." She slipped on her water buffaloes, gave her head another shake, and took the stairs two at a time.

"Mom, I'm going to be late. Where's the juice?"

"Marcella, you've got dirty streaks on your chin." That was from her grandmother. It was amazing. Half the time Grandma didn't even know where she was or what day it was, and then—bang! she would notice something like make-up on your chin. Marcy's mother flashed a warning glance; even Daddy looked up from his paper. The look said, please Marcy, no morning scenes.

"It's not dirt, Grandma." But the damage had been done.

Marcy rubbed at her chin with a napkin and felt her throat and cheeks getting hot.

Grandma Martin was off on another subject. "Someone took my pearls from my room." Her voice whined like that of a small child who had lost a favorite toy.

Marcy's mother sighed and looked at her husband for help. "Now, Mother Martin, you know nobody in this house would take your pearls."

Grandma put down her teacup with shaky hands. Some of it sloshed over the saucer onto the table. "Maybe someone came in through the back door. All I know is that I had my pearls and now they're gone."

Marcy tried. "Grandma, no one can get in the house. We have a burglar alarm. If anyone broke in, the police would be here in five minutes."

But Grandma had already forgotten about the pearls. "Marcella, I'll read to you tonight before you go to sleep. Remember how we read together when you were a baby?"

Marcy's patience was wearing thin. "Thanks, but I'm getting a little too old for that. I know how to read myself now."

Grandma Martin looked bewildered. "Too old? Then I'll make you some of your favorite cookies. The ones with poppy seeds. The moon cookies."

"Oh no," Marcy's mother interrupted. "No, Mother Martin, you are to stay out of the kitchen. Last time you tried to make cookies, it took three days to clean up."

Marcy grabbed her notebook from the kitchen desk. "Well, I've got to go. So long Mom, Dad. Bye Gram. Mom, I'll be home around 5:30. We're going over to Diane's after school."

Marcy's mother pushed back her chair with an angry scrape. "Diane's house? Oh no, you're not!" All the cheerfulness was gone from her voice. "I told you Monday, you'll have to come right home from school today. Flora's off, and I'm playing in the quarter finals of the city tennis tournament. Somebody has to be here with . . ." She didn't finish the sentence but looked pointedly in Grandma's direction.

Marcy's stomach tightened. Without answering her mother, she opened the side door and slammed it behind her. She hadn't gone five steps before she heard her father's voice. "Marcy, come back here. We've got to have a little talk."

It was no use. There was going to be another fight. They had had nothing but "little talks" since Grandma Martin had come to stay.

He closed the side door behind him. "What is the problem with you?"

Marcy's head shot up. "With me? There's no problem with me. It's you and Mom. Nothing's been the same since Grandma's been living here."

"I know it's hard. It's been hard for everyone, especially your mother. But it won't be much longer."

"That's what you said three months ago!"

Grandma was much older than the grandmothers of Marcy's friends. Marcy's father, her only child, was born when Grandma was forty-two years old. When Grandma Martin had lived in her own home, it had been lots of fun to visit. She was a great cook and loved to bake. She kept a large white porcelain cookie jar filled to the brim. Sometimes there were sugar cookies, sometimes cinnamon drops, but most often there were moon cookies. Those were Marcy's favorite. They were made of a hard, crispy dough sprinkled with poppy seeds and cut out in the crescent shape of a quarter moon. Marcy used to nibble them from all sides, trying to keep the shape of the moon until the very last bite.

Nice memories, but Marcy was sixteen now. During the last few years, Grandma Martin's health had failed. Grandpa Martin died, and Grandma became forgetful. She started wandering around town. One day the police found her miles away; she said she had gotten lost. Another day a neighbor found Grandma asleep over a cup of coffee; she smelled gas, checked around, and found the pilot light out on the stove. After a few such incidents, Dad and Mother decided she couldn't live alone.

But the nursing home in town had a long waiting list, so Grandma Martin had come to live with them—until the home had a place for her. A two-week visit had turned into three months, and no one knew how much longer it would be.

The big problem was The Rule: Grandma was never to be left home alone. It *was* hardest on Marcy's mother; after all, she had to spend most of the day with Grandma. But it was hard on Marcy, too. Sometimes Grandma would forget how old she was, like this morning with the bedtime stories. Other times she would remember and scold Marcy for being sloppy or not combing her hair. Flora, the housekeeper, took care of Grandma during the days she worked. But on the days when Flora was off and Mom had to go out, it was Marcy's turn to Grandma-sit. And Marcy Martin didn't like it one bit.

"Marcy, I'm talking to you."

Marcy's father had that pinched, tight look on his face. He must feel rotten, she thought. After all, the cause of everybody's problems was Grandma, and she was *his* mother.

"Your mother has been in all week. This tennis tournament is very important to her—she's excited about winning her first three matches and she *must* play this afternoon."

Marcy kicked the step. "But Dad, we were all going to Diane's to finish making posters for the rally Friday night. They're counting on me to do the lettering."

Dad had run out of patience. "Marcy, I'm not asking you, I'm telling you. Why don't you bring the girls over here?"

"Because, Dad . . ." Marcy stopped. She didn't want to hurt her father's feelings by telling him some of the silly things that happened when Marcy brought her friends home. It was embarrassing! Even if they went to Marcy's room, Grandma wouldn't leave them alone. Sometimes she would yell at them to turn off the records, even when they weren't playing music. No way would she bring the kids here again.

"Do I have your word, Marcy, that you'll be home?"

"Tell Mom I'll be here." Marcy started back down the walk.

"Marcy." It was Dad again.

Marcy didn't turn around. "What's the matter now?"

"Nothing." His voice was softer. "I just wanted to say thanks for understanding."

Now Marcy really felt like a rat. Was it so wrong of her to want to have her own fun, her own life like the other kids? Why is it *me* who has to be stuck with a crazy grandmother? she thought as she got on the bus.

Marcy met Diane, Sue Ellen, and the other girls at her locker. Well, I might as well get it over with, she thought.

"Diane, I can't come over this afternoon."

The girls interrupted their conversations and all began talking at once.

"But Marcy, you promised . . ."

"We've got all the poster paper . . ."

"And the paints . . ."

"You promised to do the lettering . . ."

Diane spoke for everyone. "I know, you have to stay with your grandmother again!"

Marcy's face got hot again. "Yes, my mother's in a tennis match, so I've got to get home early."

Sue Ellen made a face. "What a pain, Marcy. Your mother doesn't have to play tennis, does she? Anyway, your grandma's her responsibility, not yours."

"Sue Ellen, Mom's cooped up all week with Grandma; she's entitled. Listen, I'm sorry. What do you want me to do?"

Diane shrugged. "All right, Marcy, forget it. But I just want you to know that Doug and Eric and a bunch of the guys said they'd stop by on the way home from basketball practice."

"Gee, that's great," said Sue Ellen. "Marcy, *Doug* will be there! You've been dying for the chance to talk to him."

The bell rang. The girls said good-bye and hurried off to class. Marcy opened her locker. Not only was she going to miss a session with the girls, she was going to miss Doug Arnstead, too. And that was a big deal. He knew who she was. Marcy knew he had even asked Diane about her. But so far that was it, and she was getting anxious. Now he was stopping by Diane's—Marcy's big chance—and she was going to be a no-show. It wasn't fair. She slammed the locker. It shut, then sprang open again. A sheaf of history notes fell out. It was going to be one of those days.

Three o'clock came very slowly. Marcy's algebra assignment had been all wrong. In English she couldn't answer a simple question, and her stumbling made the whole class laugh. She had banged her hip on the uneven bars in gym, and by the end of the day, she was so upset she felt like crying.

The bus ride home was quiet. Diane's stop was first, and as the girls got ready to get off the bus, she leaned over and whispered in Marcy's ear, "Listen, I'll call if Doug comes over. Maybe your mother will change her mind and stay home."

"I doubt it, but thanks, Diane."

Marcy's mother was waiting by the front door. When she spotted Marcy, she ran down the walk, carrying her tennis bag.

"Marcy, you're a doll. Right on time." She leaned over to kiss her. Marcy pulled her face back. "Where's Grandma?"

"As a matter of fact, she's sleeping. She didn't nap at all today, so you should have an easy time. She should sleep for an hour at least."

"Terrific! What can I do while she's sleeping?"

"Do? What do you mean, do? Do your homework, play some records, read a magazine, watch TV, do anything you want. Just *don't leave the house!* Oh, set the table at 5:30 and turn on the oven. I have some baked chicken all ready to be heated for dinner." Marcy's mother started the car and blew another kiss through the open window.

"Hey, Mom. Good luck! Bring home a trophy."

Mrs. Martin beamed and hit the horn in a paradelike salute as she drove out the driveway.

Marcy kicked open the door and felt the glumness redescend as she entered the house. "Sure, I can do anything I want except go to Diane's and talk to Doug."

After helping herself to a glass of milk and a peanut butter sandwich, Marcy tried the TV. Nothing on but quiz shows and old reruns.

She opened her algebra book, but shut it after one look at the assignment for the night. She peeped into Grandma's room. Yep! She was sound asleep, her glasses next to her on the night table.

The phone rang.

"Marcy?" It was Diane. "What are you doing?"

"Well, Diane, right now I'm eating my second piece of peanut butter bread, and by the time this afternoon is over, I will probably have gained 500 pounds."

"Guess who's here, Marcy."

Marcy put the knife down. "You're kidding!"

"Nope. Doug Arnstead, among other famous basketball stars, is sitting in my den right now drinking some gross pink potion that Sue Ellen made."

"Oh no!" Marcy hadn't really believed that Doug would stop at Diane's house. There had been so many afternoons he had promised to be there—just her luck he had to stop by today.

Diane continued, "Guess what. He asked for you."

"Did he really, Diane?"

"Yep."

"C'mon, what did he say?"

"He said, 'Where's Marcy? I thought she was always over at your house.'"

"What did you say? You didn't tell him I had to be home with my grandmother, did you?"

"Of course not! Do you think I'm an idiot? I just told

him you had to stop home for a while and that you might come over later."

"Well, I can't leave."

"Maybe your mother'll be home early."

"No, she won't be home till supper."

"What's your grandmother doing?"

"Right now she's sleeping."

"Well, why can't you come over?"

"Diane, you know I'm not allowed to leave her alone."

"Yes, but if she's sleeping, what harm will it do? Come for an hour."

"I can't."

"Well then, twenty minutes. Marcy, what's going to happen in twenty minutes?"

"I don't know." Marcy clicked the receiver down. She paced back and forth and looked in on her grandmother again. She hadn't moved. Usually when she fell asleep like this, she was good for a couple of hours, Marcy decided. She locked the back door, checked the pilot light on the stove, and wrote a note in large block letters: GRANDMA, I'LL BE HOME IN 15 MINUTES. READ YOUR PAPER. MARCY.

After a quick look in the front hall mirror, she dashed down the steps and ran the three blocks to Diane's house.

At first no one noticed her, there was so much talking and laughing going on. Then she spotted Doug. Sue Ellen was perched on a chair right next to him.

"Hi, everybody."

The babble stopped for a half minute, and everyone turned to say hello. Diane gave her a little squeeze.

"C'mon, Marcy, over here. Okay, gang, Marcy's going to do the lettering for us."

Someone gave Marcy a black marking pen and pushed a large piece of poster paper in front of her. An orange-and-brown basketball was already pictured on the paper.

"Now Marcy will do some of her famous lettering."

Marcy pressed quickly and surely on the pen. The kids gathered around the desk. Doug Arnstead was leaning over the back of her chair. She began lettering, spelling out Millburn High School with curlicues and flourishes. Just as she finished the H, Doug spoke. "You're really great. I don't know why they don't give you the student council signs to do as well."

Marcy blushed. It was working. Doug Arnstead was noticing her, she was thinking, as she started to become aware of the violent whine of a fire engine. Something clicked in the back of Marcy's head; her hand trembled on the letter I. First she heard the engine noise, then a police siren and the whirring whelp of the town ambulance. Sue Ellen looked out the window. "Must be a fire someplace. Looks like they're going toward Parkview Terrace."

Parkview Terrace was Marcy's street. All of a sudden the click in her head became a pounding. She dropped the pen and pushed the kids aside.

"What's the matter, Marcy?"

"I've got to get home."

Diane nudged her in the side. "Now, Marcy?" She gave Marcy another significant push in Doug's direction. The sirens in the street grew louder.

"Diane, my grandmother! I left my grandmother alone." There was panic in her voice as Marcy opened the door and ran toward the sound of the sirens.

Her feet barely touched the pavement; her heart beat in time with the pounding in her head. She saw the fire engines, the police cars, people starting to gather. It was like looking through a reverse telescope. The faster she ran, the farther away the street seemed to get.

Her throat was dry, but her hands and the back of her skirt were wet with sweat. The pounding in her head brought back pictures she had almost forgotten. Grandma Martin holding out the huge Tiny Tears baby doll that Marcy had wanted when she was eight. Mom had said it was too expensive, but Grandma had stroked Marcy's hair and said that every little girl should have the doll of her dreams. At ten she had had a bad fight with Diane, and Grandma had let her cry her eyes out on the big over-stuffed sofa. When the tears stopped, Grandma had fixed her a glass of iced tea and let her suck a cube of sugar through her teeth as she drank it—a habit Mom and Dad considered disgusting. Even after Grandma became forgetful, she always remembered Marcy's birthday and picked out something special.

Marcy ran faster. She was almost home. There were people all over the street. Marcy prayed in rhythm as her feet hit the sidewalk. "Please, God, don't let anything happen to Grandma."

Smoke curled in the air and Marcy tripled her speed. The smell reminded her of the time she had burned a batch of moon cookies in Grandma's old kitchen. She had forgotten to grease the pan, but Gram hadn't even scolded her. She just opened a window and scrubbed the tin cookie sheet. Even when Grandpa had walked in sniffing, "What's burning in here?" she had just smiled and told him to go back to his paper.

Marcy could see people on the front steps of her house. Her legs were trembling, her vision blurred with tears.

But suddenly she saw what was happening. The people weren't looking in *her* house, they were using her steps and lawn to get a better look at something next door.

It seemed that the Rapps' garage had caught fire. Their car was parked down the street, so it was okay, but half the garage was gone.

Marcy pushed through the crowd and ran into the house. "Grandma, Grandma, where are you?" There was no answer. "Grandma," she was screaming as she ran through the house. "Grandma, it's me, Marcy. I'm home." She pushed Grandma's door open. There was Grandma in her rocker, with her apron over her head and her hands over her ears.

"Oh, Grandma." Marcy pulled the apron down and hugged Grandma with relief.

"Marcy?" Grandma had a puzzled, scared look in her eyes. "Marcy, there was so much noise, sirens, whistling. I thought the war was starting." Marcy held the frail body that was trembling like a frightened child's. How many times had Gram held her in the same way, when she was little, to soothe her fear or sadness?

"No, Grandma." Marcy smoothed a lock of hair that had become twisted in Grandma's eyeglasses. "It was a fire next door, but everything's all right. No one got hurt." She gently led her into the kitchen. "C'mon, I've got an idea."

An hour later Marcy's mother burst through the front door. The fire engines were still next door wetting down the roof. "Marcy, Mother Martin? Is everyone all right?"

Marcy yelled back, "We're in the kitchen, Mom. Everything's fine." Marcy's mother entered the kitchen. Grandma Martin was seated at the kitchen table, wearing one of her huge embroidered aprons. In front of her was a mixing bowl. She was stirring with one hand and sprinkling something dark into the mixture with the other.

"Marcy, what on earth are you doing?"

Marcy turned back from the oven, where she had just popped in a baking tin. "Mom, Grandma and I are making moon cookies."

"Moon cookies! How could you do that? We don't have poppy seeds or baking powder or . . ."

Marcy held up a mix for chocolate chip cookies. "We had this. Grandma's adding the chocolate chips. But I did find Grandma's old cookie cutter." She pointed to a tray of crescent-shaped dough pieces.

Mrs. Martin grabbed Marcy in a tight hug. She squeezed once for thanks and once again just for love. "Thank you," she murmured against Marcy's hair.

Grandma Martin looked up from her stirring. "I don't know why there's so much talking in my kitchen." She pointed to Marcy's mother. "Kate, you'd better get Hank's supper ready. And Marcella, don't forget to grease that tin real good." Marcy and her mother winked at each other, and over Grandma's head Marcy made a peace sign with two floury fingers.

King of the Hill

*T*HE PHONE WAS PERSISTENT. Linda clicked the OFF button on her electric typewriter. "Hello." Darn. The reference book slid off her lap.

"Hi, Lin? It's Heidi. You busy?"

"Heidi, I'm trying to finish my history paper."

"You're not finished yet? It's due tomorrow. Gosh, I would have sworn you'd be finished twelve hours after it was assigned."

"As a matter of fact I was. I'm just typing footnotes."

"Oh. Lin, I've got to talk to you."

"Heidi, absolutely not tonight. I've got to finish, and I didn't even wash my hair yet."

"I'll be right over."

"Heidi, have a heart." Too late. The phone clicked down. Linda smiled. You couldn't call Heidi a fair-weather friend. Rain or shine, whatever the time, if she felt she needed you, she was there.

Linda walked into the kitchen. She heard the front door open. Heidi knew about the extra key hidden behind the mailbox. She should know. The girls had been friends since they were four.

Heidi blew a kiss to the den, where Linda's parents were watching TV. "Hi, Mr. and Mrs. Grant. Everything okay?" Heidi didn't walk, she bounced on her toes and left a trail of invisible energy sparks in her wake. Completely at home, she strolled into Linda's room and flopped across the bed. "It's time we did your whole room over." Her arms waved over the flowered wallpaper, the collection of seashells Mom and Dad had brought back from vacations, and the little pink dressing table whose cotton skirt matched the canopy of the four-poster.

Linda laughed, though she felt a prickle of hurt. "Tonight? Did you come here to tell me to do my room over tonight?"

Actually Heidi was right. Linda looked around the room. A few minutes ago while she was typing, the room had seemed snug and warm—comfortable. Now she could see that it was a corny, little girl's room, not meant for someone who was sixteen.

Linda sat in a pink-and-white antique rocker her mother had refinished. A lot of love had gone into this room, and maybe that was why Linda resisted suggestions to change it. But now that Heidi had rejected it, the room itself seemed to shrink in embarrassment.

"Okay, Heidi, what couldn't wait until tomorrow?"

Heidi threw her blond hair over her shoulder in a swift, confident move that made Linda check her own reflection in the mirror. How come Heidi always looked so great? Linda suddenly realized she was doing her envy thing again. She'd thought she was finished with these feelings. She had made peace with herself since the bitter year when she was thirteen, becoming fourteen. It was then that she realized that her brown eyes were not going to turn blue and her impossible, curly hair looked awful bleached blond (a disastrous experiment, done with the help of Heidi, that took six months to grow out). Linda believed, really believed, that looks didn't make any difference in life, but somehow when she looked at Heidi, she believed it less.

Now she studied Heidi's flawless cheeks and wondered idly what it would be like never to have had a pimple. Heidi could devour pizza, cupcakes, and a malted in one sitting and still zip up the tightest jeans in town. To be best friends with a girl who never drank diet soda was really a test of character.

Heidi had been talking the whole time, using her hands to explain her words. Linda snapped to attention when she heard the final sentence. "So, Lin, I've decided to run and I want *you* to be my campaign manager."

Linda stopped rocking. "You're kidding!"

"Why should I kid about something like this? I've been talking to a lot of kids, and they think I'd have a good chance."

"Heidi, student council president is a heavy thing. You've got to run meetings, meet with the principal, represent the school in the community, keep everything going."

The blue eyes looked as if they were going to tear. It reminded Linda of the time in third grade when someone other than Heidi had almost been picked to play the princess in the class play. "Linda, you sound as if you don't think I could be president. I'm hardly the moron of the western world."

That was true. Heidi had her share of brains; her marks were good. But something intangible had started Linda's stomach churning at Heidi's announcement. Was she jealous? She hadn't been jealous when Heidi had been picked as a cheerleader when they were freshmen, or prom queen when they were juniors. As a matter of fact, she was always at her side, to help in any way she could.

There was a game they had played as kids, called King

of the Hill. You tried to claim a territory, a mound of dirt or a rock pile. One group was on one side and one on the other. You had to fight your way up the mound and push the other side off. Linda always played on Heidi's side. She was strong and could elbow kids out of the way so that Heidi could climb over the obstacles and take the title.

Well, that was a long time ago, but times hadn't changed that much. She couldn't be jealous. No way. She didn't compete in Heidi's arena. Linda looked at the brown-and-white laminated certificate that hung over her pink dressing table. It might be a bit out of place among the ruffles and flowers, but strangely enough it was the one thing that really belonged in the room and to Linda. It read, "First Prize, Kiwanis Essay Contest. LINDA SUE GRANT for her essay, THE AMERICA OF HOPE!"

Next to the award was a framed letter from the Women's Club, informing the township that Linda Sue Grant had been picked as outstanding teenager for the month of November for her volunteer work at the Senior Citizens Center. It also noted that she was a reporter for the Hillside High newspaper, *The Cannon*.

Heidi reached for Linda's hairbrush. "Look, Lin. I've been noticing things around school lately and talking to kids, and I think there should be changes. As student council president, I could make them."

"I never knew you were interested in school politics."

Heidi brushed with a practiced rhythm. "Do you know there has been a male president of the student council for the past four years?"

"So, it's been a boy. The captain of the cheerleaders for the past four years has been a girl. The captain of the twirlers is a girl, and the band drum major is a boy. So what's the big deal?"

Heidi put the brush down. "You know what I mean. The cheerleaders are girls, the presidents are boys. Everyone has been playing a role. And I think it's time we girls got together and reversed it."

"It seems to me, Heidi, that you've always been happy with your role!"

"What do you mean by that?"

"Well, I didn't notice you turning down the junior prom queen role. Why didn't you suggest a boy for the part? And why don't you quit the cheerleaders if you feel they shouldn't be girls? I assure you, there are about a hundred other girls dying to take your place."

"Boy, Lin, why are you getting so angry? I thought you'd agree with me. You're always talking about women's rights and stuff."

"Yes, but you're not. As a matter of fact, I can't figure out what you're talking about. I don't think you know either."

"Don't you see, Linda? It's my platform. I'm going to prove that Hillside High is definitely a downer for girls. We're always stereotyped."

"How did you arrive at that conclusion? And don't tell me that the school nurse is a woman, please."

Heidi began to pace. "Take the girls' gym for instance. It's in the old building, right?"

"Right!"

"The gym is dull, gloomy, the floor is uneven, the bleachers are awful, and we won't even discuss the locker room."

"So?"

"So, the boys' gym is in the new addition. It's shiny and bright, has a great locker room and bleachers, and is used 100 percent by the boys."

"So?"

"So! Why should the girls be stuck with that gross secondary gym and the boys have all the new stuff?"

Linda stood up. "Say good-night, Heidi." She propelled Heidi by the shoulders through the door.

Heidi pushed Linda's hands down. "Come on, don't you think it's a great idea? The strategy is simple. But I need you to write and direct the campaign."

"Good-night, Heidi. I'm not even going to answer you because I think the whole thing is stupid." Linda opened the front door.

"But Lin—the school has more girls than boys. With this platform I'm a shoo-in to win."

Linda slammed the door. She opened it again and was tempted to shout, "What about all the girls who won't vote for you, because you've won every beauty and popularity contest since you were in kindergarten?" But she stopped herself.

At the second slam Mr. Grant walked into the living room. "What's all the noise, babe?"

"Election time for student council president. Heidi's thinking ahead. It isn't enough that she'll probably be senior prom queen; she wants to crown herself, too."

He laughed. "Well, good for Heidi."

"How can you say that, Dad? She should no more be president than I should be Queen of the May."

Mr. Grant patted Linda's shoulder. "And that's your problem. You set limits on yourself. Who says you can't be Queen of the May?"

Linda ran up the stairs. "Because I know what I can

and can't be." She slammed the door, walked over to the dressing table, and furiously pulled blond hairs out of her brush. "Now what did I get so mad at Dad for?" she wondered, suddenly ashamed.

The next morning Linda could sense the school buzzing. Heidi was waiting outside her locker. "Hi, Lin, did you think about it?"

"I thought about it."

"Well, will you be my campaign manager?"

"I'm still thinking."

"Okay, but here's my petition. I wanted you to be the first to sign it."

Linda dashed her name off quickly. Why was she getting angry again? It was business as usual: Linda Sue Grant supporting Heidi Olen for student council president. What was any different from proposing Heidi for the lead in the Christmas play, or lending her a new sweater before Linda had a chance to wear it herself, or even clearing her path so she could be King of the Hill?

"Lin, I really need you for campaign manager. You know I'm right about the gym." Those blue eyes could smooth sandpaper.

"I'll be late, Heidi. I'll let you know later."

David Avery and a contingent of junior guys were in front of Linda's homeroom.

Dave held out a piece of paper. "Linda Grant, you are going to have the honor of being the first of your sex to sign my petition for student council president."

"I don't believe it." Linda shifted her books to her hip. "Dave Avery?" She looked at Eric Gold, who was leaning against the door. "What about you, Eric? Since you're vice-president now, I was sure you'd try for the top."

Eric shrugged. "With Heidi running on a male chauvinist platform, we thought Dave would have a better chance of pulling the girls' votes away."

David Avery was captain of the basketball team, had led Hillside to a state championship, and had the blackest eyes of any boy Linda knew. Other than that, she couldn't think of one thing that qualified him to be council president.

She stretched her arm out to clear a path. "You're too late. I've already signed Heidi's petition."

"We thought you, of all the girls, would have an open mind." That was from Eric.

"Me? What about you, Eric Gold? Talk about sellouts." She pointed to David. "Why don't you just roll over and bark when Dave Avery tells you to?"

Dave pushed his way to the doorway. "Look who's talking. Heidi pulls you out of her deck like the ace of spades whenever she needs you." Linda walked away, her throat choking with unsaid words.

The day dragged. While changing classes, Linda was approached by girls for or against Heidi and equally vehement guys for or against David.

After school there was a meeting of *The Cannon* staff. The newspaper reporters themselves were split in two. Linda was ready to leave. She was sick of hearing this all day. "Do you mean to say this is the only news our staff has to discuss? Other things are happening in this school."

She was interrupted by Cindy Blaine, a sophomore. "It isn't just the election, Linda. Heidi has brought out some important points, and Dave is trying to smear her."

Linda spoke up. "Why is everyone making such a big deal out of . . ."

Cliff, an angry senior, shouted her down. "Because this is the first time a girl candidate has come up with a flimsy platform and accused the school of being sexist."

Cindy jumped up. "Heidi's right. Look at the gym we're stuck with."

Cliff pointed a bitten-down pencil at her. "What do you think brings extra money into the school? Sporting events. *Boys'* sporting events! Basketball, wrestling . . ."

"Not so." Another girl jumped up.

Linda doodled in her notebook. Finally Mr. Spencer, the adviser, flashed the two-finger peace signal for quiet. "You're not going to convince one another by shouting. Why don't we put some of this great journalistic energy to work?"

Jody Allen, a senior and the editor, nodded. "Mr. Spencer's right. We have an editorial page on which to analyze the news as we see fit."

Cliff spoke up. "We can all submit an editorial, have our own vote, and publish the piece we think comes closest to staff opinion." Everyone agreed.

That evening Heidi called. "Lin, yes or no? You've had time enough to think."

Linda twisted the telephone cord. She didn't recognize her own voice, or maybe it was the words she didn't recognize. "Listen, Heidi, I wish you all the luck. I'm sure you'll make it. But I think I've got to pass on being campaign manager."

In the days that followed, the arguments raged through the hallways, cafeteria, locker rooms, and of course the gym. Heidi had a picture of a dilapidated, spider-webbed gym on her posters, with the caption, "WHY SHOULD THIS—BELONG TO MS? Vote HEIDI OLEN for Student Council President!"

The boys went wild with David's posters. One pictured a bat and ball dressed in lace panties and ruffles, with the caption, "I really have nothing to wear!" Another showed a basketball hoop with a fancy hairdo; it read, "I'll be with you soon as I fix my hair" and "Girls in the Kitchens and off the Courts!"

The cafeteria became a battleground as tables appeared labeled HIS, HERS, HEIDI'S GIRLS, and DAVE'S BOYS. Linda grew irritable. She snapped at everyone. To make things worse, Heidi greeted her every morning as if nothing were wrong, as if they were still the same close friends. And Linda found herself missing being on the right side of that bouncy walk.

The night before the editorials were due, Linda closeted herself in her room, thought hard, then forced herself to write. The next afternoon Mr. Spencer read everyone's piece aloud with no comment. Linda's was last. When he finished, it was very quiet in the room. Everyone turned to look at Linda. Jody spoke up. "Unless I'm wrong about the vibrations here, I don't think we need a formal vote. Linda has said it all."

The silence was broken by staff congratulations. The release of tension was refreshing. Jody banged for quiet. "The editorial will appear Friday. I'm sure I don't have to remind everyone about our policy of secrecy until the whole school receives the paper."

On Friday afternoon papers rustled as the students turned quickly to the editorial:

STUDENT COUNCIL ELECTION
TURNED INTO SHAM

The students of Hillside High will go to the polls in two weeks to elect a new student council president. We are sorry to report that the two candidates, Heidi Olen and David Avery, have turned the office and election into a sham. The hottest issue seems to be the fact that girls use

the *"old" gym and boys use the "new" gym. One of the
candidates wants to reverse the so-called inequity. Heidi
wants the girls to have the "new" gym, while David is just
as strong for keeping the status quo.*

*It does seem unfair that the girls should have all their
gym classes in the "old" gym, but perhaps a compromise
is in order. The freshman and sophomore guys and girls
should have gym in the "old" gym, while the juniors and
seniors would meet in the "new" gym. This would share
the facilities according to seniority, not sex.*

*But to the root of the problem: The Board of Education
has been trying to sell a bond issue to the voters to build
an addition to the high school. We propose that the students, under the leadership of the student council president, get behind this issue as a positive force and go out
into the community and convince our parents and other
voters that we need new facilities. We of* The Cannon *newspaper see no indication that either candidate would be
able to represent the school in this way.*

LINDA SUE GRANT, Junior Class

Linda reread her words as they jumped off the newspaper columns. It sounded so silly now! Why did it seem
so brilliant the night she was writing it?

Linda felt eyes on her as she gathered up her books after
her last class. There were murmurs as she walked by. Heidi
stopped her in the hall. There were two bright spots high
on her cheekbones.

"Lin, I want to talk to you."

"Listen, Heidi, I'm sorry if you're upset, but I had to
write it the way I felt. I tried to tell you the first night
you said you were going to run."

The spots faded in and out on Heidi's cheeks with every

word. "Oh, I don't care about your editorial so much. I'll still win. But the compromise was such a great idea. Why didn't you give it to me in the beginning?"

Now Linda felt her own cheeks growing red. "You mean you don't really believe all your slogans about the girls' gym and everything?"

"Sure I do, it's just that your ideas would have made a better platform. I wouldn't have had to split the vote between girls and guys. That's why I wanted you as campaign manager. I knew you'd come up with something. Do you think I can switch to your compromise now without losing votes?"

Linda felt her anger leave in one spurt, like air leaving a pricked balloon. Heidi was fine. She could swallow her pride and change her mind if she really thought it was necessary. She wanted to do what was right. She would probably still win the election.

All Linda said was, "I'll see you tomorrow, Heidi."

As Linda walked to the front exit, she noticed a crowd of students on the steps. A couple of them were carrying "Heidi and Dave" campaign posters. The printed sides were crossed out, and on the clean sides was written, "WIN WITH LIN—LINDA GRANT FOR STUDENT COUNCIL PRESIDENT!" A cheer went up the minute they saw her.

Cindy Blaine jumped out in front of the group and dangled a piece of white paper under Linda's nose. "Lin, since the kids read your editorial they want you to run for president."

"Me?" Linda's voice sounded as if it were being squeezed out of her throat. But as her voice quavered, an excited glow began at her toes and raced through her body. "Me?" she questioned again.

"We want to circulate this petition to get your name on the ballot."

Linda's heart was pumping as she looked at the excited group around her. For one moment she hung suspended— the energy sputtering around her, waiting for her to grab hold. In a split second nagging questions ran through her mind. What if I lose? What if Heidi never speaks to me again? What if the boys get mad? What if . . .

It was no use. The excitement was too catching—and with it came another question: What if I don't run? I'll never know if I could have made it or not!

This time her voice was firm, though her hands were shaky.

"Okay. Circulate the petition. If we get my name on the ballot, we'll give it a try!"

The group crowded around, slapping her back, reaching for her hands and shoulders, all talking at once. Linda felt a surge of confidence as she looped her arms through Cindy Blaine's and that of an unknown sophomore boy. For once she was going to see what it was like to be King of the Hill!

Next of Kin

I HAD FINALLY TOLD THEM. Everything was out in the open. I felt as if my hands were shaking, but they were pretty steady as I refluffed the pillows on the couch and carried the coffee cups into the kitchenette. Mom always wore a lipstick much too dark for her; red tracings were all over the rim. She had been tight-lipped and white when she left the apartment. Daddy had been tense, too, and there had been a droop to his shoulders as if he didn't have the strength to hold them straight anymore. I hadn't realized how badly they would both react. Now my hands did shake as I ran the cups under the water. The things we had shouted at each other. . . . But Danny was worth it— Danny of the dark hair and dark eyes and oh-so-gentle touch, Danny Donato, who was moving in with me tomorrow.

"I knew when you didn't go away to college that this is what you two were planning," Mom had shouted when I tried to explain.

Carolyn Brandt and Danny Donato. We had been a twosome all through high school. Oh, I had gone out with a few other boys, but I always seemed to come back to Danny. I just felt so safe with him, so together, as if all the things that ever bothered me in the whole world were all right when I was with him. Everything was fun.

Danny had graduated two years ahead of me and was studying at New York University. I had convinced my parents that I didn't want a faraway campus school. "Let me go to New York," I had begged. So they agreed. I was accepted at N.Y.U. too, and shared a small apartment with a girlfriend in Greenwich Village, the area of New York that surrounds the university. I was also lucky enough to get a part-time job in one of the Village bookstores. Everything was within walking distance.

Danny shared a small place with two fellows just a couple of blocks away, and we saw each other constantly. Finally it just seemed the right thing to do. Live together. We weren't ready for marriage yet.

"With every advantage you were given, this is how you're ending up, living with someone in Greenwich Village." That had been Mom's cry.

"Why don't you get married if you can't live without each other?" I had thought Daddy of all people would understand. He always took my side when Mom got emotional.

How can you explain something like this? "Daddy, it's because I want to finish school and have a career that we're not going to get married. Danny wants me to have every chance, too."

"Sure," Mom yelled, "he'll have someone to cook and clean for him, and what if you have a baby?" I didn't even bother to answer that one. It was obvious that she didn't think I was old enough at eighteen to know about anything.

My roommate Gail had been great about the whole situation. She was moving in with two other girls, and her stuff was in cartons in the living room waiting to be taken out. The closet was open. I shut the door, but after looking at the empty space for a moment thinking, Tomorrow! Tomorrow Danny's clothes will be hanging here next to

mine. Danny's shoes will be lined up on the floor next
to mine. Danny's toothbrush and my toothbrush will be
together. And on and on and on. It gave me the shivers.
Danny. No more arranging schedules to see each other,
trying to get off work early to meet for a quick sandwich
or catch a movie. No more trying to find places for our
roommates to go so we could be alone. From now on I'd
come back to the apartment and he'd be waiting for me.
In the morning we'd leave for school together.

Danny was pre-med, in a special six-year program. Next
year he'd go directly into med school. I was a philosophy
major. Eventually I wanted law—passionately, ever since
I had first watched a courtroom TV show.

The phone rang. "Danny?"

"Was it terrible?"

I started to cry. "Oh Danny, worse than terrible."

"I knew I should have been there when you told them."

"That wouldn't have made any difference. But even
Daddy . . ." My nose was running. I didn't realize how
much I had wanted my parents to approve.

"I'll be right over."

"But Gail's coming back in a few minutes, and I thought
you had to work until midnight."

"That's okay. I can get Joe to cover for me for an hour."
Danny had taken a job parking cars in one of the large
open-air lots on Sixth Avenue.

I just had to comb my hair and put cold water on my
eyelids to try to take out some of the red. It didn't really
matter. When Danny arrived he just held me close and
everything seemed worth it—even my mother's parting
words: "Don't expect any money from us to help you with
a living arrangement we don't approve of. We'll pay your

tuition as promised, but this," she pointed to the four walls of the apartment, "let your live-in take care of this."

Daddy hadn't said anything about money, and that frightened me. My part-time job helped me with clothes, and I had a partial scholarship so my tuition was all right. But my parents had been paying my share of the apartment rent. I hadn't expected them to stop that.

"It'll be okay," Danny said. "Don't worry. It'll all work out."

First thing in the morning, he moved his things over: a carton of books, a duffle full of clothes, his desk, desk lamp, and stereo.

"We can always hock a stereo if we get into trouble." I had one too, a graduation present. It was almost funny. We'd have to be on a really strict budget and learn to eat all those filling and cheap casserole dishes featured in the women's magazines, yet we both had hundreds of dollars worth of stereo equipment.

My friend Gail and Steve, one of Danny's ex-roomies, brought us a bottle of domestic champagne; I mixed it with orange juice, and we had a toast. Gail popped English muffins into the oven and I guess that was the equivalent of a catered wedding breakfast. For a moment I remembered a little girl planning a wedding, with a groom who was going to cut a towering sugar-iced wedding cake that would release hundreds of doves dyed pale pink and blue to match the rest of the wedding flowers, and a honeymoon cruise to some enchanted island.

But here was Danny, and here was I, and we were really in love, and nobody waited for fancy wedding ceremonies anymore. And we would get married someday—when he was through med school and I finished law school.

"We love each other. We're committed to each other," I had said to Mom.

"How can you consider yourselves committed when you won't get married?"

"We don't need a piece of paper to prove anything."

"You're too young." That was from Daddy.

Danny grabbed me for one quick moment and pulled me into the bathroom. He gave me one of those special kisses, the kind that sent the blood skipping from my head to my toes a half dozen times.

"Hey, lovebirds," yelled Steve, "I hate to break this up, but Danny has lab in twenty minutes."

I had to leave, too. No classes, but I was due in the bookstore for inventory this morning. Danny had to work tonight after class, but then he'd be home.

After work I hurried back to the apartment. I was in the middle of a term paper but found it hard to concentrate. I had left a notice on the bulletin board at school offering to type research papers. Typing was one of the high school electives I had done best in. I was fast—and accurate, too. Lots of students and faculty members paid for these services. I flipped on the switch of my typewriter. Darn, I hit a key by mistake. Mom hadn't been impressed by my idea of typing for money. She kept saying I was immature and used to having everything done for me. My hands sweated over the keys. "And who bought you this electric typewriter, I'd like to know?" she had said. "I didn't notice you offering to type to earn one last year. Not a secondhand portable, but a brand new deluxe model to help you with your work."

How long did you have to keep saying thank you for things? I appreciated everything they had done for me, but they just didn't or couldn't understand about Danny.

I got about three quarters through my paper and then Gail called.

"What time is Danny coming home tonight?"

"Not until eleven."

"You sound down. Everything okay?"

"*You* know. My parents."

"Oh, don't worry, they'll come around once they see you really mean it."

I thought about running down to the corner and treating Danny to a nice piece of cheese, maybe some imported brie. I had some little snack crackers, and we could have some wine. No, the last time I had bought brie it was several dollars a pound. No more brie. Okay, I'd melt some American cheese over crackers in the oven. That would be just as good. I decided to scrub out the bathroom. I didn't want Danny to find even one hair in the sink or tub. Then I must have dozed off, because the next thing I knew the phone was ringing. I shook myself awake. The phone bill! Danny didn't have a phone in his apartment. Gail and I had split the bill. Rather, our parents had. Now I'd have to learn to do without a phone if we couldn't afford it.

"Is this Carolyn?" It was a rich, deep voice with a Jamaican accent.

"Yes."

"You don't know me. I'm Joe. I work with Danny at the lot."

I sat up now. I remembered Danny talking about Joe. They usually wound up on the late shift together. They covered for each other on coffee breaks and long supper hours. Sure, it was Joe. He was probably going to let

Danny come home early tonight. I looked at the clock. It was nine already.

"Yes, Joe. Danny's spoken about you."

"Well, look, they just took him to St. Vincent's."

For a moment I couldn't think. The only St. Vincent's I knew was the hospital. I think I let out a shriek.

"You mean the hospital?"

"Now don't worry. Danny was complaining all night. He said he'd been sick in school, too, and then he doubled over, so one of the guys took him to the emergency room."

I don't think I said thank you or even hung up the receiver. I just raced out the door, without even throwing the double lock, and was down the street. I do remember the chill in the air; I hadn't even stopped to grab a sweater. St. Vincent's was in the Village, right around the corner. What could have happened? Hit by a car? No, Joe said Danny had doubled over. He had been fine this morning. . . . Then I remembered he really didn't drink the champagne, just took a sip; he had classes and didn't want to get spaced out, he said. Had he looked a little pale? Tired? Come to think of it, last night, when we had ordered in pizza, I remember he had moved the pizza around on his napkin and hadn't eaten much. He said he thought he had a touch of stomach virus, something going around.

I ran straight to the emergency charge desk. "Just brought him in, you said?" the white-capped nurse asked. "Just a minute, I'll look. Are you a relative?"

"Yes, I'm . . ." That stopped me. I didn't know what to say. Technically I wasn't a relative. I mean, I guess a wife is a relative, but of course I wasn't a wife, and I certainly wasn't his sister.

She was waiting. "I'm a close friend."

"Look, I have to page a surgeon right now; we have a stab wound that's bleeding all over the place. If you're not next of kin you'll have to wait."

I guess I must have looked sick because she picked up the phone and called for the surgeon and then searched through the white sheets on the desk. "Yes. Daniel Donato, brought in at 8:37. He's in cubicle six, but you can't go in. The doctor's with him."

"What's wrong? Will the doctor talk to me when he's through?"

"I don't think so, only members of the family. Sorry, honey, we're just too jammed with patients to hold the hand of anyone who comes off the street to visit."

Anyone! I wasn't *anyone!* I was the most important person in Danny's life, and he in mine.

I squeezed in next to a mother who held a screaming baby in her arms. The baby's eyes were running with a yellowish pus, and the mother kept saying, "Please, nurse. Please, nurse. Where's the doctor?"

It really panicked me. I waited until the nurse was busy with her paperwork and then made my way past the desk to the back cubicles. There was just a curtain strung across the opening of number six.

"Danny?" I whispered.

"Carolyn?"

"Don't move." I heard a voice and realized it must be the doctor.

"It's my girl. Can she come in?"

I didn't wait for the yes. I know that "white as a sheet" sounds trite, but that's what he was, white as a sheet. He tried to lift his hand, but I could tell by his grimace that he was in too much pain. A doctor and a nurse were inserting I.V. tubes. I just stood at the foot of the table. His jacket and shoes were on a stool in the corner, and silly as it seems, I started to gently rub the soles of his feet—just to touch him and make sure he was all right.

"Out of the way a minute, miss."

The doctor was adjusting the I.V. flow.

"Pain, terrible pain."

"Sh." That was the nurse. "Don't try to talk." She turned to me. "Are you a member of the family?"

Again that question. Danny's voice sounded so weak. "Don't laugh, Carolyn, but would you believe they think it's an ulcer?"

"Ulcer?"

"Yeah. I guess too many pepperoni pizzas."

"We've got to get him upstairs. His blood count's dropping. We'll know more of what's going on later."

The desk nurse walked in. I thought she'd yell at me, but all she said was, "Does he have insurance? Where is his Blue Cross and Blue Shield card?"

I didn't know. I had only been in the emergency room of a hospital once when I was about seven for a cut finger, and then my mother and father had taken care of everything.

They were starting to wheel Danny out. "Where are you taking him?" I asked.

"Upstairs."

"Wait a minute," the desk nurse said. "He's got to sign this—permission to treat. He was unconscious when they brought him in."

Unconscious. Permission to treat. Danny's eyes were closed; maybe he was out again. "Can't I sign for him?" I asked and grabbed the pen.

"Are you responsible for him? Next of kin?" They all looked at me, and I slowly handed back the pen.

Danny opened his eyes. "Student at N.Y.U. I've got insurance." He coughed and groaned at the same time. "Give me the pen." I should have remembered about our student insurance. The nurse held his head up while he signed, his fingers falling to his side at the last scrawled O.

"Carolyn?" He opened his eyes. "Wait for me, I'll be right back."

I followed as far as the elevator. The doctor was young; he had nice eyes. "Listen, are his folks near by?" I nodded. "You'd better call them. He might need surgery. Don't worry, Dr. Peters is on tonight for all gastro cases and he's tops. But he might need transfusions, and the family is going to be responsible for replacing all blood used."

The elevator closed as Danny managed what looked like one last encouraging wriggle of his toes for me.

I tried to find out where they were taking him. All I got in answer was "upstairs." The charge nurse did stop and ask me if I knew who the next of kin were so they could get in touch with them. I remembered that line on all school forms from kindergarten on up. Next of kin. The person responsible in case of emergency.

It was me, wasn't it? I wanted to be responsible for Danny, but they weren't letting me just because of a stupid bureaucratic technicality. I could still hear one of my mother's arguments. "House. The two of you just want to play house without taking on the responsibilities of a real commitment to each other. You have to earn responsibilities."

I called Danny's parents and then started to cry for the very first time as I dialed my own.

* * *

It was only an hour, but it seemed like forever until the four of them arrived. My father had driven in. Mr. Donato ran up to the desk.

"Daniel Donato? I'm his father."

The charge nurse perked right up. "Yes sir, you can go up. He's on the seventh floor, room 712. Only members of the immediate family, please."

Mr. Donato put his arm around me. "She's a member of the immediate family."

Mom and Dad waited downstairs while I rode in the elevator with the Donatos.

Mrs. Donato was crying softly. "His stomach . . . he always ate junk. I knew this six-year program was too much for him. Danny always tried to crowd too much in. And what did he need that parking lot job for?"

For me, I wanted to say, but I couldn't. We hadn't told Danny's parents about our living arrangements, and I realized that no matter how angry my parents were they hadn't said anything to the Donatos.

"We never knew Danny had an ulcer." If only Mrs. Donato would stop crying! But then my own throat was backed up with an ache that I knew came from swallowed tears.

I did remember lots of stomachaches, even in high school. Stomach viruses, Danny always said. I'd visit him at home, usually sneaking in some candy and a stack of magazines, and we'd laugh and I'd plump the pillows behind his head and he'd call me his nurse. Playing nurse, I guess, just like we were going to play house.

The doctor met us at the door to his room. "He's okay. We've stopped the bleeding. This is a warning, and he's had a good scare. He's going to have to watch his diet and get lots of rest. He's not out of the woods yet. The most important thing is he's going to have to learn to slow down and not get into any stressful situations."

Thoughts flashed through my mind—crazy thoughts that scared me, made me want to run away. I couldn't stop them, either. It was too much responsibility. What did you feed someone who had ulcers? Cottage cheese, I think, and lots of milk. I wouldn't be able to throw spicy little casseroles together. Danny would have to give up the parking lot job. That was too much for him with his studying. Professor Miller had told me I'd have a chance at a working fellowship this summer if I could produce a really outstanding research paper. How could I take on extra typing, keep my bookstore job, take care of Danny, and work for my fellowship? It wasn't fair. Why did this have to happen? And then I realized that I was whining—yes, whining just like a child, but in my own head.

I took a deep breath before we entered the room. I knew we couldn't talk now, but Danny and I would have to do some reconsidering. I loved him madly, and I knew he loved me, but I guess it wasn't enough to be just a live-in playmate, and neither of us was ready to take on the responsibility of a next of kin.

Another Blue-Eyed Quarterback

*S*TEPHANIE OPENED THE WEEKLY rambling letter from Mom that ended with the usual admonitions, "Are you eating, taking your vitamins, keeping up with your work, wearing an extra sweater, and writing in your journal? Remember, all writers keep journals," and so on. Stephie didn't even have to read it. She knew the litany by heart. It was nice to know that her parents hadn't changed. Everything else seemed to have. Three months at Crestview College in Vermont and she could have sworn that the world was flat instead of round, that autumn leaves were falling up instead of down, and that she was a transplanted weed in this garden of blooming golden girls.

Was it only last year that she had been a high school senior, yearbook editor, co-captain of the majorettes, with a fantastic best friend, Dena, to confide in, and of course Chad? Just saying his name to herself still hurt. Chad Leighton, with the blue eyes and strong shoulders that had carried him to the other end of the continent on a football scholarship. Chad, who had promised to write and remain true. Well, he had written once—no, twice, really. The first was a postcard saying that things were great but football practice was rough. The second was a letter after she had written about twenty-seven times, telling her that they were young and he didn't think he'd be home for winter vacation, and maybe next summer. . . .

And now the letter from Dena, who had quit nursing school. "Bed pans, temperatures, enemas—not my *bag* (if you'll excuse the pun)." Before she had signed off with a row of typewritten Xs along the bottom, Dena had confessed that she was in love—*again*! She also told Stephanie not to break her heart over Chad. "After all, you're only seventeen." And P.S., she had reminded Stephie that there were other fish in the sea, birds in the sky, and even more blue-eyed quarterbacks around.

Stephie could hear rock music and laughter from down the hall. The girls were in Doreen's room again. They had invited her, but she just couldn't seem to get into things at Crestview. The girls were so different. They had asked her outright, the very first night, if she were a virgin, if she "did" pot or any drugs, and a hundred and one other intimate questions. Maybe they thought she was a snob for not answering, but then she had had Chad's picture to dream over when she felt homesick or unsure.

There was a meeting of the literary magazine before dinner. Reluctantly, Stephanie pulled on her boots and reached for extra sweaters. Mom didn't have to remind her. It snowed early in Vermont. It almost wasn't worth the walk up to the administration building to find out she hadn't been accepted. The things that had come so easy to her in high school were really tough here. Maybe she should have tried out for the marching band. The few issues of the magazine she had read were great. The poetry alone had made her skin tingle.

She crunched up the steps toward the administration building, her breath clearing a path in front of her. The door was locked, and students were standing around stamping snow from boots and outer clothes.

Paul Darcy, a senior and editor-in-chief of the magazine, arrived and, with a great show and rattle of keys, unlocked the door. The Crestview *Tracings* was his fiefdom, and he ruled like an ancient lord of the manor.

To try out for a staff position, Stephie had filled out a questionnaire, submitted two samples of her writing, and was now ready for the interview. Last week Doreen had given her some tips. "Be assertive in your interview— though why you want to be on that magazine is beyond me. So be assertive, but don't come on like you're a big deal and know everything."

That advice circled in Stephie's brain. How could you act self-assured without blowing your own horn? Like all the advice she was receiving these days, it seemed to have a forked tongue. Last year just knowing that she and Chad were together used to give her self-confidence to spare.

Paul had on a long ski sweater over his jeans. Most of the staff imitated their chief with similar ski sweaters and jeans tucked into their boots. It seemed as though the intellectuals on campus knew enough not to get their feet wet. Stephie's jeans hadn't been tucked in, and the edges were wet where they had caught the snow. The dampness seeped into her skin. She didn't know enough to keep dry.

"Stephanie Brandt?" Paul was seated on the edge of a desk. She stepped forward and, forcing a smile, said, "Is this the way to the inquisition?"

No one laughed. Feeling rattled, she turned the smile down. "That was supposed to be a joke." No one bothered to laugh at that, either. Gosh, didn't anyone on this campus have a sense of humor? And the girls in the dorm thought she was the heavy one.

Anyway, she wasn't sure she wanted to be a writer anymore, hadn't written anything decent in months. It was easier to be a majorette; you didn't have to tear yourself to pieces. Paul had her papers in front of him. The other members of the staff were seated around the table looking solemn. He held one up. "Were you trying to be funny when you wrote this?"

There had been a special question on the application form, "If you were going to write a novel now, what would the topic be? The object of this question is to spot originality and versatility."

Stephie had answered the question in the form of a book review. It read, "*The Case of the* Tracings *Magazine Murders*, a novel by Stephanie Brandt. A mysterious fire in the chem lab, a tragic car accident. Suddenly five of the top aspirants to a position on *Tracings*, the literary magazine of Crestview, are dead. A cloud of mystery hangs over the campus. The trials of young womanhood, the terrors of competition, get to freshman Nancy Johnson. Ranked last, she sees her future in jeopardy. The quiet Vermont college town is plunged into murder and intrigue as Nancy plots her way toward the number one spot on the magazine. 'Terrifying and exciting . . .' *Newsweek*, 'Pertinent and reflective . . .' The *New York Times*. Soon to be a major motion picture."

Paul repeated his question, "Were you trying to be funny?"

It had seemed like a dynamite idea at the time. All the other applicants she had talked to were being so serious about the question. Some said they would write books that would bring world peace or solve the energy crisis, while others were toying with the idea of rewriting the Bible. She hadn't thought she was being funny so much as witty and satirical and yes, she was trying to show originality.

"*Tracings* is serious, Ms. Brandt. It isn't *Mad* magazine."

She felt the sudden warmth in her cheeks. Think of something else, she told herself. Chad. No, there were no more thoughts of Chad to comfort her, though she still kept his picture tucked in the corner of her mirror. All right. Paul Darcy has a pimple on the side of his nose. Concentrate on that.

"I thought we were supposed to be original?"

"Original, yes." Concentrate on his pimple, Stephie, she told herself.

"But junior high school jokes, no."

The others around him nodded their heads in agreement. One of the girls spoke up. "I have to agree with Paul." You would, thought Stephie. Now that he has pronounced sentence, all of you creeps will jump in.

"As for your poetry . . ." Before Paul could continue, Stephie reached for the paper in his hand.

"I think I've got the picture. You don't have to say any more." She had written the poem at the end of her senior year. No one had seen it, especially not Chad. Chad didn't like to see feelings written out on paper. It would be too much to have Paul Darcy criticize this piece in public.

He handed it to her. "Okay, but I was just going to say that your poetry is a trifle self-conscious right now, but I think it's worth working on."

She was shaking inside, but he didn't seem to notice.

"Some of your images are not my choice, however. . . ."

She continued her internal dialogue. Since they are *my* images, why would they be *your* choice?

"Anyway, we think you show promise. If you can give us some more stuff in the spring, we may be able to fit you in staff next fall."

"Thanks a lot," she mumbled, "but right now, I'm

swamped with work so I don't even know if I'll have time to get something ready by spring." She felt a catch in her throat. That meant she was going to cry soon. You all have pimples on your faces, she observed silently. And you're all horrible and ugly. Junior high jokes! I wouldn't want to be on your stupid magazine and I'll never show any more of my writing.

She put on a smile through a trembling lower lip. "Thanks a lot, but I may just be switching out of the English major, anyway."

"What would you switch to?" asked Paul.

"Well, I really want to be a nuclear physicist." There. If he thought she had junior high humor, she'd give him some. She almost swept out in a grand exit, except her scarf caught on the edge of a desk and jerked her backward with a stumble. "Sorry." She loosened herself and walked out the door.

"Hey, wait." It was Paul. The cold slapped her in the face, which was good. Paul would think the wet spots in the corners of her eyes were caused by the sudden cold.

"Don't walk so fast. I didn't think a girl who could write like you would be so damn touchy."

"Touchy? What makes you think I'm touchy?" Her voice still had that catch, and she didn't know how long she could hold back tears.

"I'd really like to talk about your poem."

"I think I got your opinion of my work."

"No, I don't think you did." He grabbed her arm. "What the heck do you have on, bandages around your arm?"

"Sweaters. It's about four degrees below, or haven't you noticed?"

"That's the trouble with you. A smart-ass freshman

wanting to be noticed. Just like your answer to the book question."

She pulled her arm away. "Before we freeze into ice statues and are bulldozed away by the maintenance department, I'd like to get back to my dorm."

"I've got to go back to the meeting, anyway. We've got a bunch of losers this time around. *Tracings* never takes freshmen, but I'll tell you this: if we did, you'd probably be the one."

"Thanks for nothing."

"You'd better do something about being so sensitive. You won't last a year if you don't toughen up."

"Thank you, but my skin is so tough now that I scrub with Brillo."

"Smart-ass." He lifted her chin with a hand that was surprisingly soft. "You're in Lawrence Hall, right?" He didn't wait for an answer. "I'll call you."

"Terrific. I'll go back to the dorm to hold my breath until you do. It'll make a great story. Freshman applicant loses breath over rejection from *Tracings* editor."

He scooped up a handful of snow and threw it at her. She turned toward Lawrence Hall, and finally the tears did start. The folder was still in her hand; she ripped it slowly, watching the pieces flutter across the snow. She imagined spring coming and the snow thawing and students finding pieces of her manuscript all over the campus and pasting them together to be published with great acclaim. One of the pieces blew back and caught on her cheek where it held, stuck to one of her tears.

She kept to herself the next few days, which was easy. Exams were near and everyone was frantic. On Thursday night she was called to the hall phone.

"Stephanie Brandt?" It was a strangely familiar male

voice. "The menu in the cafeteria tonight is creamed tuna and noodles, with a salad that was fresh when man first landed on the moon. I'm heading for the O.R. Care to join me?" It was Paul.

Stephie had to laugh. The O.R., Orchard Rest, was a small hangout off campus that served burgers and sandwiches.

"I have a paper to work on."

"I'll be at your dorm in fifteen minutes." The phone clicked before she had a chance to answer. What conceit. He was that sure of himself. She was still mumbling as she changed her sweater, ran a brush through her hair, put on and then wiped off some strawberry lip gloss.

They didn't talk much on the way to the O.R. Once there Paul ordered a beer. "One for you, too?" he asked.

"Sure." She hated the taste of beer but wouldn't let him know.

"Look, kid," he patted her hand, "I'm here on a scholarship and a writing grant. I don't have money to throw around. It's my treat tonight, so if you're not going to drink the beer, don't waste my money."

Her face turned bright red. Was he a mind reader? "I'll have a Coke." No sense trying to drink a glass of beer and throwing up just to impress this nonimpressible person.

"That's better." He ordered two burgers with the works. "Now I want to hear all about Stephanie Brandt and what makes her tick."

"I think I'll have less of a stomachache if I eat the cafeteria's creamed tuna."

"Come on, Stephanie, stop with the jokes and talk."

The food came, and for a moment she thought of the mountains of burgers she had shared with Chad. Her hand shook as she drowned her hamburger with ketchup. Paul helped her wipe some of it off and pushed his glasses to the top of his head. His hair was dark, long, and shaggy around his face, and his eyes were laughing. Stephie would have felt better if they were brown, black, or speckled—anything but that clear, piercing blue.

He asked some more questions, and before she realized it Stephie was telling him about her home and how uncomfortable she felt at Crestview and how maybe she should be a majorette at college instead of trying for a serious position on the magazine. She told him about her journals and how she tried to write something every day. Paul was leaning against the back of the booth. Stephie stopped, suddenly embarrassed. She had never spoken this freely to Chad, especially about her writing.

Paul ignored her embarrassment and started talking about his own writing: how much the magazine meant to him and how he was 300 pages into a first novel.

As they stood up to leave, he reached for his wallet. "Damn, I just realized. I don't get my check until the end of the month. How about if it's your treat tonight and I'll get it next time?" Stephie had to laugh. She had been too well trained by Mom not to carry money with her. But Paul Darcy was the most unusual person she had ever met. He didn't even say thanks when she paid the check. He just told her to make sure and leave a good tip because the waitress was working her way through college.

He put his arm around her shoulder as they walked back to the dorm. It felt good, very familiar, not like Chad familiar, but—natural, that was the word. He was talking earnestly, gesturing with his free hand, their breath intertwining like smoke circles—separate, then mingling together in a great white mist, and separating again as it evaporated into the sky.

"How old are you, anyway?" he asked.

"I'll be eighteen in two months."

He turned her around and without warning kissed her quickly on the mouth.

"You're a cute kid, you know that? Anyone else would have just said eighteen."

She was a little breathless and confused. The kiss had been so quick, and then he hadn't stopped talking. Almost as if it hadn't happened.

"I've got papers to read, so we won't go back to my room tonight. Get a rest. You look tired."

He was really insufferable. What made him think she would even go back to his room? And telling her to get a rest. She didn't have time to think anymore, because this time he pulled her close and kissed her softly. Her neck was wedged in a funny position. He sensed it and without taking his lips off hers, lifted her head and increased the pressure on her mouth. Her knitted cap fell off and she felt the roughness of his gloved hands through her hair. The kiss lasted a long time. He stopped before she was ready, picked up her hat, and playfully pulled it down over her ears.

"Stephanie Brandt, I'm gonna lose my grant if you don't get upstairs. And you fogged up my glasses." He turned away from her and walked toward the administration building, whistling.

She licked her lips. He tasted like the hamburgers, with a faint hint of beer, but he smelled kind of woodsy. That was ridiculous. Of course he smelled woodsy—they had been standing in the middle of a clump of evergreens.

She hurried into the dorm and reviewed the whole evening, grimacing to herself over every remark that now seemed silly and immature. There was a note on her door. "We're in Doreen's room. Do you have anything for the munchies?"

She suddenly felt like talking, maybe all night long. She certainly couldn't fall asleep right now.

Stephanie dropped her ski jacket on top of her books and reached for the bag of chocolate chip cookies Mom had sent. She started down the hall, whistling. The draft from the door slamming shook the pictures stuck in the corners of her mirror. A blue-eyed quarterback slipped down behind the radiator, followed by the colored tassels from her majorette boots.

The Makeover of
Meredith Kaplan

*Y*ou can't judge a book by its cover, and beauty's only skin deep. To find the worth of a person you must search deep inside. Oh sure, I've heard all these statements, plus others: having a really great personality is much better than being built, and a man wants someone he can sit down and tell his troubles to, not some dumb but beautiful blond. What do I say to all those statements? Bah, humbug! You try them out on your average gorgeous captain of the football team, especially around senior prom time!

I learned that early in life. When I was about eleven years old I heard my Aunt Doris say to my mother, "Meredith is such a kind child. I'm sure that after the braces come off and she has a good haircut she'll have her own special look!"

I guess that's what you get for listening in on conversations you're not supposed to hear. Anyway, I'm seventeen and in my senior year at J.F.K. High, the braces have been off for four years, I've had dozens of haircuts, and believe me, I'd trade *special* to hear the word *pretty* any day of the week. Of course I'd never admit it, not even to my best friend, Lisa, who is as different from me as a best-selling record. You know, she's the hit single and I'm the quiet, subdued tag-along they had to record on the flip side.

Anyway, I've really been too busy during my four years

of high school to get myself crazy over a zit on my nose, or scraggly eyebrows, or even half-bitten fingernails. With two brothers and two sisters already in college and grad school, my parents told me from the very beginning that without a scholarship my immediate future would be narrowed down to the community college in our area or night school if I worked during the day. They didn't intend to be mean or discouraging; it's just the fact of my life, and they always wanted me to face it.

So in the hierarchy of high school I guess you would categorize me as a "grind," but an active grind because I've had to go out for all sorts of extracurricular activities to round out my college applications. When colleges say they want a "well-rounded" student before they hand out scholarships, they're not referring to your figure.

Lisa and I were filling out our activities sheets one night. Mine covered two pages. I'm editor of the yearbook, which I'm really proud of, but I've also served hot dogs during halftime at the football games, been chairperson of both the spring and fall class carwash, and worked as a candy striper in our local hospital.

Here I am in the second half of my senior year, with all my college applications sent out and most of my tough schoolwork finished. So I'm able to take a breath and enjoy putting the yearbook together. It's kind of like a puzzle. Lisa likes to interview people and write things up with razzle-dazzle and then throw the stuff on my desk to lay out and organize. I guess it sounds as if I'm jealous of her. I don't like to think so, but maybe I am deep, deep down in the tiny bottom of my heart. After all, it's pretty hard not to be jealous of a Brooke Shields look-alike, dress-alike, who is also nice. It's not a really nasty jealous, just a kind of jealousy like "Gee whiz, she has so much. Why couldn't I have been given her eyelashes?" Just the top pair would have been sufficient.

As of January first all my classmates seemed to be senior prom buggy, which is premature, since the prom is in June. Of course the girls who are going with someone don't have to worry, unless the romance breaks up. The boys never have to worry; they can always ask one of the underclass girls. There are always sophomore girls batting their eyes and giggling hysterically at everything that comes out of the mouth of a senior boy. I watched all these silly maneuverings with a very superior air. Catch me worrying over a prom date? *Never*!

Lisa plunked herself down at my desk one afternoon in early March.

"We have to talk about the prom, Meredith."

"We do? Please move, Lisa, you're crumpling up the English Department." I was editing that section of the yearbook.

She slapped my hands. "Forget the English Department and the yearbook. We have to talk about the prom."

"Oh, for heaven's sake, it's three months off." It isn't as though I didn't go out during my four years at J.F.K. High. I was always included in groups. You know, the "good old sport." I went to the games and picnics, but I guess I never had what you would call a real boyfriend. Lisa always said it was my fault. Not only did I not pay enough attention to my appearance, I was always too businesslike and sharp. Well, I don't have time to be soft and kittenish and sweet like Lisa. Besides, there was always Clay Wells. He was the editor of the literary magazine and the statistician of the basketball team, and he already had a scholarship to M.I.T., where he was going to major in computers, if there was anything left about computers that M.I.T. could teach him. I guess Clay was really the stereotype of the class grind. But he was a good guy, and when people would couple off at picnics or parties we would wind up together. We would talk, mostly about the future, and Clay would occasionally try to aim a few computer-planned kisses somewhere near the vicinity of my mouth, but other than that we were strictly friends. I mean, he didn't make any bells ring or my knees turn to water, and I certainly didn't see rainbows when he kissed me good-night.

We had made a special pact. If either one of us was stuck in a situation where we needed an escort of the opposite sex, we would call on the other. Now, mostly just to get rid of Lisa, I said, "Look, stop worrying. Clay and I will go to the prom together just like we did to the junior dance and the sophomore drag."

"Aha, Miss Smarty . . ."

"Ms., if you please, and stop swinging your legs, Lisa. You're giving me a headache."

"Very well, Ms. Smarty. But please take a minute to surface through this stuff you've buried yourself under. And speaking of burying, your bangs need to be trimmed again. I told you your eyes are your best feature, and they're buried under all that hair. How long has it been this time?"

I blushed, couldn't help it. She had gotten me this time. My bangs were scraggling into my eyes. I had borrowed two clips from Barbara Ann during gym period and pinned them back. The trouble was that one clip was tortoise shell and the other bright blue, and the rubber band holding the rest of my scrags back in a ponytail was yellow striped.

"Now hear this. For the past three weeks, Clay Wells has been seeing, now get this, seeing, which means . . ." Lisa counted on her fingers, the tip of every one of which was polished with a pearly pink sheen, shaped into perfect little ovals without a hangnail in sight. I sat on my hands before she had a chance to notice that my fiftieth resolution not to bite, pick, or otherwise maim my nails was no longer in effect. ". . . two movies, cute little late night tête-à-têtes at King's Pizza, holding hands in front of her locker—her locker, mind you—Sara Woodruff."

I looked puzzled but my stomach felt a little sick.

"Sara Woodruff, junior class treasurer, blond, blue eyes, just loaded with Fair Isle sweaters that match those baby blues and with eight beads on her gold add-a-bead necklace."

I still couldn't see what she was leading up to. Of course I knew who Sara was.

"Well, accurate rumor has it that Clay has offered, and little Sara has accepted, his kind invitation to join him at the senior prom."

There were two ways I could react, and Lisa was watching me closely. First I thought, what a fink! Clay could have gone with me and we could have spent the evening drinking punch and mocking the starlight that was bound to be shining out of the eyes of all the couples. Those kids were determined to press prom night firmly into their memories as the best night of their lives, just as the girls would press their flower corsages in the pages of some thick book. Why, I wouldn't even have cared if he didn't shave too closely, or if he did and patched himself up with a wide Band-Aid. And Clay would have laughed rather than lectured me if my fresh manicure was half peeled off before we got to the punch bowl. But then, I felt kind of relieved. Underneath my mocking exterior I think I am romantic. I would like to dance away prom night under the stars with someone who could make me quiver like Jell-O, whatever that means—someone who would think I was pretty or cute, not just a really good sport and "one of the guys." Of course how could you admit this to someone who looked like Lisa? It had always been so easy for her. Even when she was little, she was what everyone referred to as a beauty.

I'm just as nice a person. The trouble is that people look first before they decide to get to know you. And now apparently my friend Clay, who had always seemed to share my scorn for the dating practices of our peers, had himself fallen under the spell of two blue eyes and a shape that could fill an ad for jeans!

"Well, I shall just have to find someone else. Of course I could always go stag and stand behind the punch bowl and serve. Or visit my grandmother in Cleveland a little early."

"Oh, come on, Meredith, quit joking. It's probably the best thing that could have happened. Now you'll start thinking seriously about a date for the prom."

"Right now I'm afraid, Lisa, I shall have to copy a phrase from Scarlett O'Hara and 'think about it tomorrow,' because I've got lay out the ad pages. The sponsors are coming in at a terrific rate."

And so with my usual good humor, I managed to change the subject around. The next couple of weeks passed quickly, but I began to notice that Clay was different. Oh, we still kibitzed and joked with each other when we passed in the halls, but the first thing I noticed was his chin. No more gucky-looking Band-Aids stuck all over.

One day he asked me to read his history notes. I looked around to see where that spicy smell was coming from. Then I realized that Clay had on after-shave lotion! And his favorite brown-and-tan lumber shirt was pressed and tucked into his jeans, which were belted with wide, dark tan leather and a large gold clasp. And for the first time in about four years, I actually saw his ears, because his hair had been clipped neatly around them.

"Clay, are your eyes blue-green?"

"What did you say, Meredith?"

"Your eyes. I don't think I ever noticed them before. Your glasses! What happened to your glasses? You can't see three inches in front of you without them."

"Contacts." He lowered his head and blushed. "It took me a few weeks to get used to them, but now they're great. My parents gave me an early graduation present. Do you like them?"

He actually had thick, curly lashes, almost as long as Lisa's.

"Well, it must be terrific to be in love. Did Sara cause all these changes?"

"No, not exactly. I thought I'd just kind of change my image, to get ready for college next year. Listen, about Sara. I know we always had this understanding about sticking together for special dances and things."

I held up my hands. "Say no more, Clay. I'm sure that Sara's very sweet and I suppose it's good for everyone's morale to have a real date."

"Thanks. And listen, my cousin Ned lives in Irvington. You remember him? I could always get him to take you to the prom."

Strangely enough, my eyes filled with tears and I had to

blink quickly before they spilled over. "Hey, no sweat. If and when I decide to go to the prom, I'm sure I can arrange my own date."

"Hey, Meredith, don't get mad. I just don't want you left out."

"Don't worry about me, Clay Wells. I'm sure I can get a date, and without spraying myself to imitate a spice cabinet."

"Oh, my after-shave. Do you like it? Sara said it was her favorite scent."

"Later, Clay." And off I stalked down the hall, trying to decide why I felt so darn upset.

Lisa and I had to go to the shopping mall that Saturday. We were trying to collect more ads for the yearbook by visiting merchants in person.

There was a huge crowd standing under colored balloons and banners in the middle of the plaza on the first floor. Lisa and I edged our way through to see what was going on.

"Oh Meredith, look!"

A small stage had been set up with tables and chairs arranged around the edges. There were six young men and women fussing over girls who were seated in the chairs. The loudspeakers were blaring out music.

"It's a makeover," Lisa shouted above the din.

Then I noticed the posters. "*Today's Teen* magazine is in Millburn to make over twelve lucky young ladies."

"Oh, isn't this fun!" Lisa pushed me in closer 'til we were right against the stage.

It was littered with blond, black, and all shades of red hair that had been clipped from the heads of the girls sitting in front of the tables. Some were having make-up applied, eyebrows tweezed, their hair set in hot rollers or blown free. It was as if a bunch of magicians were hovering over the stage. Their liquids and powders were magic potions, and hairbrushes and scissors were turned into magic wands.

The audience was full of oohs and aahs, and even I was fascinated at the transformations taking place.

"Miss, oh miss, could I speak to you for a minute?" Lisa was trying to get the attraction of one of the cosmeticians. What would she ever want to be made over for? I thought. What more can you do with perfect? Then I realized.

"Oh no, Lisa. I know what you're thinking. Absolutely not. Do you think I would make a public display of myself?"

I don't know what happened. I tried to get away but I was hemmed in by the crowd. Lisa spoke to someone important, one of the tables emptied as a newly transformed Cinderella left the stage to applause and cat calls, and I found myself in the still warm wooden chair. A cape was tied under my chin and a hairdresser called over. There was a standing mirror in front of me. I tried to tell myself this wasn't happening. I felt like Alice when she'd just fallen down the rabbit hole.

After a quick look the hairdresser soaked my hair with water and began clipping away. The cosmetician dipped cotton and sponges into all kinds of liquids and oils and spread them on my face.

Lisa was yelling encouragement from the sidelines like a cheerleader. I tried to close my eyes, grit my teeth, and think of two hundred and seven ways I would personally maim, torture, and finally kill Lisa when I left the platform.

After what seemed like hours, I opened my eyes to hear the cosmetician's instructions. "We've written everything on this sheet of paper for you. You have beautiful eyes and absolutely gorgeous cheekbones. If you keep your eyebrows cleaned of all those extra hairs, your make-up will show. Come on, look in the mirror. Carlos just used a blower on your hair. You have a great natural wave."

Natural wave, beautiful eyes, gorgeous cheekbones, could they actually be talking about Meredith Kaplan? I looked in the mirror expecting to see one of those painted china dolls with ruby red cheeks and thick goopy eyelids. But there was an absolutely dynamite-looking girl, and it was me! It was Meredith Kaplan. I know, because I saw the tiny round birthmark under my left eye.

My bangs were trimmed and tapered and the rest of my hair had been layered. It fell back from my face in soft, feathery waves. I have brown eyes, and they had been accented with a little bit of pale green shadow and brown mascara. My eyes were sparkling and shiny, out from under the thick eyebrows that used to run together across the bridge of my nose. There was just a little bit of blush high on my cheekbones, and with the faintest pink gloss my lips looked actually kissable.

"Shake your head back and forth," instructed Carlos. I did and watched my hair spin out gently and fall right back into place perfectly. "If you have a good cut, your hair will always look like this."

Before I knew it I was descending the steps, instruction sheets in hand, and this time the applause and whistles were for me.

Lisa raved and raved. I walked gingerly through the mall, stopping now and then to look at the sleek and pretty, that's right, *pretty* image that stared back at me from the store windows.

"I knew there was something under all that. Meredith, you look absolutely wild. Wait until the kids in school see you."

I was happy that she was raving but also felt that I must have been an absolutely number one slob in my "before" period, which was approximately sixty-seven minutes ago. My chest puffed out as I began to float along. Why, with my looks and my "nice" personality, there probably was no male who would be immune to me for long.

"When I think of those wasted years, I could cry," said Lisa.

I didn't tell her, but I was thinking the same thing. Where had I gotten the idea that all attempts at self-improvement were strictly for the vain and the frivolous? I had spent most of my high school days with only one of my oars in the water—when I, like everyone else, had two to paddle with!

I soon realized why the Fairy Godmother gave Cinderella a 12 o'clock curfew after her transformation. It's pretty hard to be a princess twenty-four hours a day. First I had to cope with my family's reaction. As an indication of their astonishment, my sister Sally gave me a small bottle of her very favorite lily of the valley perfume. "It would have been wasted on the old you," she said.

The kids in school were equally astounded. I found myself running into the bathroom between periods to make sure I still had on lip gloss or that my mascara hadn't smeared. The first night I washed my new hairdo I had been really frightened. How would I ever get it to look the same? I needn't have worried. It wasn't as perfect as

Carlos had done it, but I managed to flip it back into place with my hairbrush. Being beautiful became a full-time commitment, and I didn't have time to think of a wisecrack or something funny to keep me in the public eye.

When Clay and I met for our weekly study period, he was mesmerized. "You look fantastic, Meredith. And what do you have on? Now *you* smell like a flower garden."

Hmm. One for me, I thought. Let him tell good old Sara that. Quite a few boys who wouldn't have looked at me at all except to say, "How you doing, pal?" now stopped at my table in the lunchroom to talk.

I went out with Michael Brady about three times. He wasn't exactly the captain of the football team, but he was still part of the popular crowd and very good looking. Then on our fourth date, over pizza—which I didn't dare eat because it would have smeared my lips—he asked me to the prom. "That is, if you don't have a date."

This was it, the high point of my life. I should have been in ecstasy, but I wasn't. Of course I accepted and, since it was now April, breathed a sigh of relief that I could finally relax and let June come.

Lisa was overjoyed and began badgering me over the gown I would have to buy for the big night.

"Oh, give me a chance to relax. I've got my sister Sally's gown. My mom said she'd fix it for me. You know we have a tight budget."

Lisa frowned. "Well, I wish you could have your very own dress, but I guess it'll be all right."

Michael and I were together every Friday and Saturday night. I wish that I could say he was my Prince Charming, but I don't know, something was missing. All we ever talked about was the other kids, who was going with whom, what we would do at the prom, after the prom, and before the prom, and about the engine of his car. His kisses were nice, but I still didn't feel like Jell-O or rainbows or swinging garden gates. As a matter of fact, I yawned a lot.

At the end of April, Clay and I held our last study session. We were all alone in the classroom.

"Gee, I'm going to miss this next year when I'm at M.I.T."

"Miss what?" I looked around the room. "This smelly old school?"

"No, not the school building, but being with you these four years, studying. We've always had so much fun together."

Suddenly I realized that I would miss him, too. Good old Clay, we always had so much to talk about, laugh about. I reached for his hand to give it a gentle pat, somewhat like the way you would show kindness to a favorite pet. As my fingertips brushed his, I felt it, just for an instant. Then he grabbed my hand in his and reached over and kissed me right on my kissable lips. And then I knew he must have felt it, too: a tiny tingle that began in the tips of my fingers and ran up my shoulder and right down my spine to the tips of my toes. I tried to shuffle my feet and then I knew what it meant to have your legs turn to Jell-O. There was a soft, warm feeling all through me, and I gently pulled back to look at Clay.

"Your glasses are fogged up," I said. Then I looked again. "Hey, where are your contacts?"

"Oh, my eyes were a little irritated this week, so I've been giving them a rest."

He also had a Band-Aid on the right side of his chin where he had cut himself shaving, and his short-sleeve shirt wasn't pressed. I nuzzled up to his cheek, sniffing. It didn't smell like spices anymore, but there was a nicer, better smell of soap and light sweat and Clay. Yes, he definitely smelled like the Clay I used to know.

I shook my hair out of my eyes and realized it had been six weeks since my makeover and that I hadn't gone back for a new haircut. I had also been in a rush this morning and left home without my blushed-on cheekbones, and my kissable lips must have been really kissable because I had lost the tube of lip gloss three days ago.

He kissed me again, and I tried to decide what tune the bells that were ringing through my head were playing and to enjoy all the colors of the rainbow that danced behind my closed eyes.

"You're terrific," he said.

"I know," I said.

"What was that?"

"Nothing, just keep kissing."

"Meredith, will you go to the prom with me?"

"Yes," I said. "Except I have a date already."

"I know," he said between kisses. "I have a date, too."

"We'll work it out," I said.

"You'd better believe it," he said. And then we didn't say anything at all.